LOVE, SEX & THE WRONG BRIDE

PRAISE FOR *LOVE, SEX & THE WRONG BRIDE*

"Wonderfully funny and terribly true." —*Fay Weldon*

"Urban, hip, sad, funny, a tipsy walk on the wild side."
—*Malcolm Bosse*

"Subversively funny and fresh." —*Publishers Weekly*

Katia Lief

LOVE, SEX & THE WRONG BRIDE

Originally published as Peculiar Politics by Katia Spiegelman, in 1993, by Marion Boyars Publishers, London and New York

For Oliver

Acknowledgements

Thanks to Renni Browne for her early enthusiasm and guidance, to Miriam Sivan and Trudi Vogel for reading and commenting on the novel-in-progress, and to Marion Boyars for publishing it the first time around.

One

Super Lover of my Dreams

It was two months ago to the day that she came home and found the note. What a coward he was! But smart, sharp as a blade, the way he severed the bond before she realized he wanted to.

> Dear Dawn,
> I don't know how to tell you this, so I'll just say it: I'm leaving. I love you. I also love her. I may not be brave, but I like to think I'm honest, and I cannot continue living a double ~~lie~~ life. I will always love you. I think I will miss you. Please do not blame yourself. Here is a check for $636.82 to cover my share of next month's rent and utilities (projected) for the balance of this month.
> Love,
> Hank

Dawn folds the letter — typed neatly on Hank's company letterhead — slips it back into her wallet and stashes her purse in the bottom file drawer. She sits back in her swivel chair, behind her desk piled with papers and manuscripts and phone messages, and does not even contemplate work. *Why does she still love him?* The jerk! But the point is, she does, and she wants him back, and today she feels inspired. It could be the toasty late May morning. Or maybe it was last night's dream: there is Hank, on his knee, in front of an arbor covered with white lilies and pink roses, begging her back; and there she is, in a flowing white dress, knowing in her heart that she can't refuse him; a crowd of people cheer and clap; and a bridal bouquet comes sailing right to her. Sometimes dreams tell you messages, sometimes they give you hope, sometimes they totally mislead you. In this case, Dawn takes the hope and the message and disregards the chance that it could be her mind playing a hoax. She decides to shed the anguish of the past two months and — woman, seize the day — call him.

Hank marches into his office and drops his briefcase on the desk with a *thlunk*. His furious green eyes go cloudy and confused. He grabs the phone and presses it to his ear. 'No,' he says to himself, 'don't.' He slams the receiver back in its cradle, and freezes. Indecision. Fury. Humiliation. He can't move. He sits stiffly in his burgundy leather chair, his hands flat on the desk, his glazed eyes staring blankly into the middle of the room.

There is a brisk knock on the door and Carla, his secretary, pokes her head through. Why doesn't she just leave him alone? Especially this morning, after. . . . No, he refuses to think about it. What is she staring at?

'Coffee, Hank?' she says. A smile animates her plain, wise face. She is an intuitive caretaker, experienced in support, with a native though somewhat inarticulate intelligence. With some education and encouragement, she could have been running neck-and-neck with him for the partnership he's after.

'Bring me two,' he says.

Her eyebrows arch.

Ignoring her, he snaps open the latches on his briefcase.

Carla departs with a slight, but detectable, slam of the door. The moment she has gone, his hand reaches for the receiver. And again he stops himself. Instead, he lifts the top of his briefcase and peers inside at the neat stack of papers, which he had brought home to work on last night. Did he work? No, no way, not with Chris prancing around distracting him. How is he supposed to defend his client if he can't concentrate on his work? After, after ... he can't stand to think about it. About her. He holds his hands to his head, as if it's about to blow off, and remembers that he left the apartment without brushing his hair. He can feel the kinky mess of how it dried, unbrushed, on his way to work.

He has always known that someday, somehow, Chris would undermine him. And this, he is sure, is just the beginning. Or maybe it started a long time ago, when she came between him and Dawn. Why did he ever leave Dawn? He can't remember a single incident of anger between them, not the solid kind of frustration he gets with Chris. The snitty, sexy, lewd . . . his neck relaxes and he shakes his head and takes a deep breath. Chris is never boring and that was what attracted him in the first place. But now she has begun to exhaust him. She is draining the energy he used to put into his work, and he is beginning to feel the pull of a slow downward curve, an incremental arch, barely noticeable as it's happening but leading ultimately to failure. Some mornings now, when he wakes, he is surprised to find that his first thought is that he is a doomed man.

Doomed.

This morning, that damned hairspray misfiring over her shoulder, shooting him right in the face. All so she could get her hair to wave and lilt in the right directions. He barely knows what her hair looks like without being encased in all that goop. Is it blonde, naturally? Who knows.

Hank can still see her face in the mirror when she screamed. Her bright fuchsia lips stretched into a big O and her blue eyes bulged. She looked ridiculous, really laughable, and he told her so. He said, 'Woah, you look like some kind of clown,' and then he had the nerve to laugh at her.

That was when she turned around and gave him another squirt in the face.

'That's it,' he said angrily. 'You're nuts!'

'Go to hell, Hank, just go right to hell!' She grabbed her jacket and her bag and stalked past him towards the door.

'Where are you going?'

'To the magazine. Where do you think?'

'Damn it, Christine, you could have blinded me.'

'So sue me.'

She stood there like a prima donna, sexy and mad in her billowing white silk blouse tucked into a tight white miniskirt, with her hands on her hips and her fuchsia nails pressing into her waist.

'Forget it,' he said, his anger dispersed in a cloud of lust. He closed his eyes and leaned forward to kiss her; but instead of her lips, he felt the sharp slap of her palm on his cheek. The door slammed shut. He opened the door and lunged into the hallway. There she was, waiting for the elevator, her blue plastic bookbag slung over her shoulder.

'That's it.' he said. 'No more.'

She pursed her lips and stepped into the elevator, leaving him with a sassy look that said *oh yeah?*

Thinking about it now makes his heart race. He comes to the office to work, not run the endless loop of his conflicts with Christine. Why, when it comes to this woman, does his intelligence become so dangerously obscured? He knows that what he needs now is distance and time to think, evaluate and decide the course of his future, with or more likely without her. He decides, in that moment, not to go home tonight. He'll call Andy and see if he can stay there.

Carla brings two cups of coffee with milk and carefully sets them down next to his briefcase. Then she digs into her skirt pocket, pulls out a red plastic comb, lays it next to the cups and leaves.

She's right, of course; his hair is a mess. But he doesn't need Carla to tell him so. He doesn't need any woman to tell him anything. They should all just leave him alone, he's a man with work to do. Jabbing the intercom button three times, he demands not to be disturbed for any reason other than a call from upper management or his new client. Thus cut off from the world, reality, and particularly the women who rule his life, Hank drinks his coffee, combs his hair and plunges into his new case.

At one o'clock, Carla brings in his messages and announces, 'I'm going to lunch.' She's mad at him, he can tell; and now that he has calmed down, he feels guilty. He takes the pile of message slips and smiles with attempted warmth. 'Thanks,' he says.

'Uh huh.'

'Sorry about before, Garla, I —'

'Dawn called,' she says.

Obviously she thinks he was a real jerk about Dawn. He clearly remembers Carla's reaction when he called her into his office to dictate the letter announcing his departure. She slapped down her pen and said, 'Wait a minute, Hank. Are you serious?' He remained poised, and continued. After a few moments, her shorthand resumed. She did not speak to him for the rest of the day.

He says, 'Take a long lunch.'

'I will.'

He looks at Dawn's name spelled out in Carla's neat script. She checked the box for *call,* which he normally takes as an unquestioned directive to pick up the phone and dial. Certainly, he knows both Dawn's numbers by heart. But to dial Dawn would be to summon the combination to a locked Pandora's box full of unfinished love and unredeemed guilt. He had walked away not knowing how to handle it, figuring actions spoke louder than words, even though these actions were driven by confusion and words may have healed him and saved them. Why is she calling now? Is she finally going to blow her stack about the cowardly way he left her two months ago, packing a suitcase when she was working late one night and leaving the letter for her to find when she got home?

He cannot bring himself to call her. Work, he thinks, concentrate on *work.* He has a new client, a tough case which could earn him the coveted partnership if he does well. He has got to prepare before meeting Mike Blitsky for the first time tomorrow.

Hank is intently scrawling notes on a yellow legal pad when his phone rings. Carla's still out to lunch, and his phone keeps ringing and ringing. Finally, he answers it: 'Henry Lowe.'

'Hank.'

'Dawn?'

'Hanky!'

'Dawny!'

'How are you, Hank?' She sounds civil.

'Great, everything's fine. You?'

'Oh, terrific'

Now he hears the distance in her voice. No confidence. Something is wrong.

'Are you sure?'

'Of course.'

'Work okay?' he asks.

'It's fine. In fact, I just got a new assignment, my first major book.' Dawn is an Associate Editor at WeatherhofF. 'How about you?'

'Great. Work's great. I'm getting closer to making a partnership, I think.'

'So, is there any chance you could meet me for a drink after work? I guess we can't do dinner.'

Chris. But he is not going home tonight, maybe not even tomorrow night. He can do dinner if wants to. But does he?

He says, 'A drink would be nice.'

They meet at a bar in midtown, with a pink neon sign shining PLANET EARTH into the dark street. Dawn spots him immediately, standing by the sizzling neon, peering in. She can see the tension in his face. His evening stubble accentuates the squarish jaw and hides the dimple in his right cheek, camouflaging him as a tough guy, when she knows he is soft.

His auburn hair has a kink she does not recall. He looks sexy, large, powerful, a good-looking man obsessed and burdened. He takes work too seriously to realize that he could be happy if only he allowed himself to disengage from the phantom pressures of responsibility that gird him.

Hank feels a clamp on his forehead and a thousand butterflies in his stomach. When did he last see Dawn? It had to be when he went back to their apartment to pick up his things. He sees her waiting for him at the end of the bar, punctual as ever. He's ten minutes late. Squeezing by a man seated next to her, he kisses her cheek. 'You look great,' he says. And she does. He forgot how pretty she was: big hazel eyes, curly golden hair, peachy skin and that smile — sad and friendly at once. She is wearing the five-strand choker of freshwater pearls he gave her on her twenty-eighth birthday, three years ago. He had just landed his job and was feeling prosperous and lucky.

'You look terrific, Hanky,' she says. The smile broadens, she shakes her head. 'Really good.'

Hanky. That's what she used to call him. He feels like her brother, and for now, after this morning with Chris, it feels good.

'I ordered a beer for you,' she says.

'You were sure I'd be here.'

'I didn't think you'd stand me up.' She takes a sip of her red wine.

How could she be so sure, after what he did to her? He knows they're both thinking the same thing: about two months ago, about now, and about how for the first time in years they don't know what's happened in each other's lives in between. They have lost the strand of their ongoing dialogue. He notices the faint white line around her ring finger; not enough time has passed for that memory to disappear. Last March, in a warm burst of pre-spring sunshine, they spent an afternoon on a windy beach. Both were sunburned by evening. He had given her the diamond and emerald ring that morning, and she returned it by mail just a few weeks later. Why hadn't he been able to go through with it? He had found a good and beautiful woman, fallen in love with her, proposed. Then Chris. What was wrong with him? Chris had broken right through his barrier and made him raw with need. He wonders if Dawn knows he slept with Chris five times before they broke up, instead of the admitted once. Even then he was aware that Chris knew her hand, knew that with each bout of passion she strengthened herself by weakening him. Poor Dawn, she didn't deserve it.

'What's going on?' he asks.

She forces a smile. 'Nothing. I just thought it was time to see you.'

'Tell me about your new project,' he says.

'I don't want to talk about work, really. Do you?'

'I guess not.' And he doesn't. He really wants to talk about her, to find out if she has someone new. Should he tell her he is still with Chris, that she's driving him crazy but he's too cowardly to do anything about it? No, he can't tell Dawn any of that.

So what do they talk about, Hank and Dawn, with so much between them and so much they could be discussing? They plunge into a lengthy survey of current movies. Meanwhile, they consume quite a bit of alcohol. And before they realize the significance of it — or the danger — they are gushing over each other. Hank has an arm around Dawn's waist, and she is leaning against him and even, from time to time, rubbing her soft white shoe against his grey suit leg.

'Let's go have some dinner,' he says.

'Dinner? Really? Can you?'

'I can do anything I want. I just have to make one phone call.'

It doesn't occur to him that Dawn must assume he's off to call Chris, when in fact he is calling Andy about using his sofabed that night.

Back at the bar, he says 'No luck. I'll try later.'

And she says, 'Listen, Hank, maybe you better not have dinner with me.'

'Why?'

'You know.'

'I was going to crash at a friend's tonight. He isn't home, I got his machine, so I have to kill some time. Come on, kill it with me.' He gives her that gloriously confident smile that won her vote years ago. She had always relied on his appearance of strength and direction, and now — that smile — she is just as moved as ever. And so, instead of probing the obvious — why is he free tonight; and is he really *free!* — she accepts his surface offer of the next few hours, totally hers, without complication, without explanation.

They taxi uptown for Chinese food, since she lives on the upper west side and he has to head in that direction eventually, to Andy's. They huddle together in the back seat, without speaking or acknowledging the rising tide of mutual feeling. When they reach Hunan Palace, they reluctantly disengage their hands.

As they walk through the Oriental arch leading into the restaurant, Hu, the maitre d', rushes toward them with enthusiasm. 'So good to see you,' he says. 'Haven't seen you in so long.' He ushers them to their old table, in a back corner, and stands before them, smiling. After some time of coming here together, they had stopped consulting the menu since they knew it so well. They look at each other now and smile. Hu says, 'Okay, cold noodles? Fried dumplings? General Tso's Chicken, okay? Crispy Beef?' They nod at each suggestion and he hurries off to fill their order. Surreptitiously brushing their knees together under the table, they discuss the savings and loan crisis, avoiding any mention of what is most on their minds — that old, magical entity, *us.*

Until after dinner.

'So,' she says. They are standing outside the restaurant, stuffed and sleepy and happy. 'It really was so nice to see you again, Hanky.' She smiles.

'Listen, Dawny, would you like to, you know, come up to Andy's with me now for, you know, a nightcap?'

'A nightcap?'

He smiles.

She looks right into him, and says, 'I'd love to.'

They head even farther uptown, beyond Columbia University and Barnard, to upper Claremont Avenue. There's a church nearby, and just as they get out of the cab the midnight bells start ringing. Walking arm-in-arm across the street, Dawn asks, 'Who is this Andy?'

'I met him a couple months ago,' he says, deliberately not adding that he met Andy through Chris. 'He's an investment banker.'

'It seems unusual that he would live away up here. He must have some money.'

'He's got a white guy complex, thinks it makes him seem socially aware to live on the edge of Harlem, not just another grey suit.'

They stand in the delapidated foyer of Andy's building, waiting for the elevator which finally scrapes its way down. There is graffiti on the elevator walls. Andy lives on the ninth floor where the hallway is dark and drab, lined with brown bags full of bottles and stacks of newspapers for recycling.

Andy — short, chubby and darkly hairy — answers the door wearing a bright red bathrobe that stops just below his buttocks. His thighs bulge out like sausages.

'Hey, guy.' Hank greets Andy. 'Didn't I mention I was bringing a friend?'

'Woman friend, you said.'

Hank turns to Dawn. 'Sorry.'

Dawn makes a quick secret face, ridiculing Andy.

Andy says, 'Never apologize' and leads them down a narrow hallway into the small living room. The walls are lined with prints of abstract paintings and bookshelves crammed with paperbacks. A formidable collection of records, tapes and CDs takes up two whole shelves. On a small table next to the couch is a framed photograph of a man surrounded by three small, pudgy boys.

'Andy Shoemaker,' he says to Dawn, extending a hand.

'Sorry,' says Hank.

'Dawn Waterston,' she introduces herself.

Andy looks from Dawn to Hank, who can see that the information — *Dawn* — is registering in Andy's ticker-tape mind. Please, Hank wishes, *please* don't say anything about Chris. Why did he bring Dawn here? Stupid! But Andy seems like a man's man. He won't mention it to Chris. Will he?

They share the couch and Andy sits opposite in an arm-chair, his knees spread wide. He is not wearing underpants. 'Wanna drink?' He smiles.

'I'll have one,' Hank says.

Andy gets up and goes to a low wooden cabinet. He slides open a door revealing a prolific collection of bottles. 'Glasses are under here,' he says, pointing to the lower shelf. 'Help yourselves. I'm going to bed. I have to leave at five to catch the six o'clock shuttle to D.C. Sheets are in the hall closet. Blankets, pillows, everything you need. Pull hard on the sofabed when you unfold it, it gets stuck.' He disappears down the hall and into his bedroom.

Hank pours himself a half-inch of Scotch. 'I need to un-wind,' he says. 'What a day!'

'Me too. I'm nervous too. I mean, I feel tense. Work is so demanding.'

He sits next to her on the couch and balances the glass on his knee.

'Let's trade backrubs, Hanky, like we used to.'

Suddenly, the fact that he loves her looms up from his sub-conscious, like a monster rising from depths he'd rather leave buried. He has always been a man of action; introspection disturbs him. Loving Dawn, now, disturbs him. Yet here she is, in the flesh, indisputable.

'Backrubs?' he mutters.

'Never mind. We don't have to. It's just that I thought—'

'No, you're right. I thought the same thing.' Meaning that they both thought coming here together meant they would be making love.

She takes the glass off his knee and sets it on the coffee table. 'Hank, I have to tell you, I still have feelings for you. I do. It's the truth. I just had to say it.' She sighs. 'That was hard.'

'It's okay, Dawny,' he admits, 'I feel the same way about you.'

'I *love* you, Hanky.'

They melt against the back of the couch into a luxurious kiss. The warmth and familiarity are deeply, surprisingly exciting. 'Dawn,' he whispers between kisses, 'I love you.'

They're out of their clothes in minutes. Blink. Then Dawn abruptly says, 'Wait a second.' She gets up and forages through her purse. She holds up a flat foil package.

'Condoms? But Dawny, it's me.' How could she? They lived together for years. They were sleeping together long before the world worried about AIDS.

'Hank, please. When I became single I made it a policy: no rubber, no sex. Not that I've had . . . never mind that. The point is, how do I know who you've been with? Sorry, but that's my rule.' She looks serious about it, too, sitting there stark naked, her face concerned and intelligent, nipples erect, stomach still wet from his licks.

'Okay,' he says, 'you're right.'

'Thanks, sweetheart. Don't worry, it won't hurt.' As she rolls the condom down his wilting erection, she says, 'It's only psychological, Hank. Relax. We'll get you back in action. You'll be the same old Super Lover of my Dreams.'

That's what she used to say to him. And it always worked. And it works now. Here he comes, up up up, and fully condomized they proceed. She feels like heaven to him despite the barriers of rubber and unasked, unanswered questions. He can't imagine why he ever left her.

Two

A Surprise and a Coincidence

When you're single and you come into the office in the same clothes two days in a row, it means that you, Drone, are also a Spontaneous Lover. Despite her better judgment, Dawn goes to the office in the same yellow linen skirt and white silk blouse as the day before and can't resist flaunting it in front of her co-workers: striking poses, yawning aloud, stretching. It's a false yet seductive bravado that pleases her and fools no one. Since Hank left, she has been aware of a razor's edge of insecurity always lurking nearby. Any sudden move, high or low, and she finds herself nicked, bleeding. Thus has loving Hank left her, once again: a night of him, and she is both triumphant and petrified.

After work, she takes the subway straight to Kath's. Kath Goodhue is her oldest and best friend. Dawn gets out at One-hundred-third Street and walks two blocks down until she is enveloped in the salsa music that blares from the Spanish bakery beneath Kath's building. The music snaps and swirls and Dawn can't resist dancing a few steps. She looks up and sees Dr. Johnson perched in Kath's third floor window, demurely cleaning his fluffy black face with a white paw.

'Hey, Doc,' she calls up.

Dr. Johnson stops primping, opens his round yellow eyes and tilts his face, and for a moment he resembles an owl.

Kath leans out of the window in her worn-out green terrycloth robe. Her long black hair is wet and tangled. 'Hi! Did I forget you were coming?'

'I tried to call but your line was busy and I couldn't wait. Guess what I have to tell you?' But Dawn doesn't give Kath a chance to guess; she dashes around the corner to the front door and excitedly presses the intercom. Kath buzzes her in and she zigzags up the four tenement flights.

Kath has opened her door a crack and Dr. Johnson sits there, regal and serene, waiting.

'I hate it when you leave the door open like that,' Dawn says.

Kath sits on her couch, towel-drying her hair. She smiles. A Suzanne Vega tape plays and Kath taps her bare foot to the calm rhythm. She looks pretty — delicate, long and pale. She seems relaxed. Her blue eyes shine brightly tonight. Too much studying, Dawn thinks.

'I'm not worried,' Kath says, 'I mean, if they're out there, they're gonna get me no matter what.'

'They *are* out there, Kath. You've got to be careful.'

Dawn sits next to Kath on the couch. The apartment is small but comfortable: a bedroom with a window facing south into an alley, a big old bathroom with a deep procelain tub and hand-laid black and white tiles, a tiny kitchen, and this living room cluttered with couch and table and books.

Dawn says, 'You'll never guess.'

'Then tell me.' Dr. Johnson jumps onto Kath's lap and purrs.

'Guess who I spent the night with last night?' She laughs. 'Guess.'

Kath shrugs her shoulders. 'I dunno.'

Dawn stares, smiles, nods significantly and says: 'Hank.'

Kath is surprised. 'Are you kidding?'

'You'll never believe it. I mean, okay, let me start from the beginning.' Excited, she takes a couple of deep breaths. 'I was at work, thinking about when Hank and I first knew each other, and how much we liked each other, and how good it was, and how awful it was that we lost it. And I was thinking about how much time we spent together, and what good friends we were. Plus, the other night, I had this incredible dream about us. And I thought, how can we just vanish from each other's lives? Despite everything that happened toward the end.'

'So you called him?'

'Yup. I left a message, but he didn't call back, and I thought maybe Carla forgot to give it to him. She used to do that, flake out occasionally, and it really burned him up. Anyway, I called again, and he answered, and we made a date. We met for a drink, and drinks turned into dinner, and dinner turned into the whole night.'

'But what about his —'

'He was staying at a friend's and he asked me to come over for a *nightcap.*' She laughs.

Kath rolls her eyes. Then: 'Why was he staying at his friend's place?'

Dawn is quiet.

'You didn't ask him?'

Dawn shakes her head, sighs. 'I should have, but I just didn't.'

'Remember what your old shrink pointed out to you about wishful thinking? That really struck me, Dawn. You do that, I've seen you, it's a real hazard —'

'Why do you assume this isn't real?'

'I don't assume anything, I'm only listening to you, and you just said he's staying with a friend and you don't know why. I don't want to see you get hurt again. You were devastated.'

'You're right. But Kath, I really love that man. There we were, it was wonderful. He even wore a condom because I insisted. He did it for *me.* Then, after, we just pulled out the sofabed and crawled in. In fact, I wore these same clothes to work yesterday. Everyone must suspect.'

'Are you seeing him tonight?'

Dawn shakes her head. 'No. Not that he asked me, but anyway, I don't want him to think I'm too available. I have to be smart this time. He should think I've pulled my life together a little more than, well, than I have. I don't want him to think I'm desperate. Right?'

'Right,' Kath says, and smiles.

But Dawn doesn't catch the smile, the hint of some new pleasure. She thinks, *poor Kath,* all these years of studying, so few men. No decent men, certainly, have graced her life. And she, above all, deserves it so much. Kath is so beautiful and brilliant and good. Maybe being an eighteenth century English literature scholar intimidates men, Dawn thinks, skipping instantly to the cynical refrain: but then what doesn't? Kath has been alone for a long time, and has never been willing to mold herself to any notion of what a woman is expected to be for a man, but has simply, straightforwardly been what she must be for herself. She has her work, a long-term goal to achieve something meaningful, to become a Professor of Literature. She'll scale the Ivy Leagues, where she will blossom on the academy vine. Kath, in the long run, will have her day.

'How's the thesis going?' Dawn asks.

Kath sighs. 'Up and down. Some days I'm raring to go, and other days I just can't concentrate. Those days are bad. I go to the library — the same library, day after day — and search through the same stacks — day after day — and sometimes I just can't get into it. For all the time I've spent in the library this week, I should be ready to write another section. But I'm not. I just haven't been very productive.' Her eyes twinkle. She looks at Dawn and starts to say, 'I can't focus, I —'

'Oh!' Dawn twists abruptly to face Kath, without realizing that her friend was about to tell her something important, something significant. Dawn just plows ahead without even noticing the small tight smile on Kath's face. Dawn says, 'I have an idea. I need a researcher for a book we just contracted at Weatherhoff. Maybe you'd want to do it. It would be a change of pace for you, and you could earn some money. Wouldn't it be great to work together?' Dawn is suddenly, keenly aware that her plan to help Kath will also free her own time for romance.

Kath pets Dr. Johnson with long slow strokes. 'Tell me about the book.'

'It's a co-authored bestseller about —'

'How do you know it's going to be a bestseller if it isn't even written yet?'

With a quick sigh, Dawn says, 'It's just a marketing thing. They don't really know, but they plan it out so it has every chance of becoming a bestseller. In this case it's a sensational story and the book was ghosted by the co-author who wrote that big blockbuster *Toaster Man* on the appliance salesman turned magnate. They're going to commit a good part of the advertising budget to give this book a big push. Really, Kath, I wish you wouldn't give me that holier-than-thou look. This is my career. We can't all be brilliant scholars, you know.'

'I'm sorry, Dawn. So, what's the book?'

'I mean it's not like I made publishing into what it is. It just is that way, and it was my first job, and I got promoted, and here I am now. The only way I can ever nurture undiscovered talented writers is if I first develop my career. You know that's what I'm going to do, once I get a little farther along, you know I'm going to really try to change things.' Every time Dawn thinks about the nature of her business, she flails, then gets miserably depressed. Deep down, she feels like a sell-out. So she tries not to think about it, and to move forward instead.

'It's okay, really. So, what's the book?'

'This book is my big break. If this book flies, I'll make Senior Editor in a few years. At least I'll have a chance.'

'That's terrific! What's the book?'

'Really? Do you really think so? I mean, Kath, you know I really respect you. Here you are, living here, sacrificing your whole life for scholarly endeavor. I mean, that was how it was supposed to be, in school, and you're doing it. I'm so proud of you. I have so much respect for you. Do you really think I'm doing the right thing?'

Kath smiles softly, maternally. 'Yes, I think what you're doing is just fine.'

'All right, okay. The working title is *Misled Mike Mauvais and His Marvelous Men*. It's a co-authored autobiography of a man who ran a transvestite prostitution ring. A "call boy" service. It's really amazing material. This guy, Mike, has been raking in a fortune. It's shocking how many of this city's most upstanding men used these prostitutes. We can't go into the clientele, though; that's a big drawback. But we can make intimations, push it as far as possible without naming names. Mike's a real flashy character. He has some wild stories to tell, and he's telling them. There's just one thing: he won't fess up about his past, his childhood. We're drawing a complete blank. It's like he wants us to believe he just hatched, *voila:* misled Mike Mauvais. But the reader will want to know his background — it won't be a satisfying story without it, and it is after all an autobiography — so the editorial board decided we would just go ahead and conduct some quiet research of our own. Dig up some background, if we can, then present it to him and push for his approval. Now, he once let something slip about a boyhood adventure in Bayonne, that's New Jersey. It's all we know. So I thought, okay, we'll go to Bayonne and start by checking the public records and see what turns up, if anything.'

'New Jersey? I don't know.'

'It's just across the river. You don't get out of Manhattan enough. You could use a break. Not to mention the money.'

'The money.' Kath sighs. 'I suppose I really could use it. My next fellowship check doesn't come until September. The university suddenly gets very disorganized when it comes to sending out money.'

'We usually pay freelancers a hundred-fifty dollars a day, sometimes a little more, depending on what they're doing. If you do full days, I could probably get you top dollar.

Unless you'd want to make it an hourly rate. But if you put in seven hours, and don't work too hard, the day rate comes out better.'

Kath has a big smile on her face. *'Misled Mike Mauvais and His Marvelous Men.* It sounds like an eighteenth century farce.'

'Wild, huh? I'm starved. Want to get a pizza? You know, you really should get a VCR, Kath. Then you could watch movies and order in, like normal people.'

Kath's eyes get that look, that twinkle. She says, 'What I was going to tell you, before you cut me off —' Dawn winces; she hates it when she does that to people ' — is that I met someone.'

Dawn is instantly curious. 'Who? When? Where? Tell me everything.'

Combing her fingers through her tangled hair, Kath asks, 'What time is it?'

Dawn checks her gold watch (a Christmas present from Hank, two years ago). 'Almost seven-thirty.'

'He'll be here any minute.' She stands and tugs her bathrobe belt. 'I have to get ready.'

'You have a date? Tonight?'

Kath ignores Dawn's obvious surprise. 'Why don't you stay for a few minutes and meet him?'

'Are you sure? That might intimidate him. I mean, can he handle meeting your friends so soon?'

'It's not that soon. I've been seeing him for almost three weeks now.'

'Three weeks? You didn't tell me.'

'Well, I didn't want to jinx it. Do you know what I mean?'

Yes, Dawn does. You start blabbing about a new love affair, and just when everyone has been duly informed, the guy splits, leaving you in a cloud of humiliation.

'What's his name? Where did you meet him?'

'I met him in the copy shop.' Kath smiles. 'He was reading the signboard, looking for used tools, and I was copying the first thirty pages of my thesis to show my advisor, Professor Banks. Anyway, we got to talking, and —'

The downstairs intercom rings.

'He's here.' She buzzes him into the building. 'I'll get dressed. Will you let him in?'

Of course, Kath knows that Dawn will be only too happy to meet, greet and assess her friend's new love interest. She rushes into the bedroom and slams the door.

Hmm, thinks Dawn, *tools.* Does he work with his hands professionally or as a hobby? If Kath likes him, he must be an intellectual. Mustn't he?

The doorbell rings. Dawn tucks her blouse into her skirt, rakes her fingers through her hair and clears her throat. She swings open the door, quickly smiles and says, 'Hi, I'm Dawn, Kath's friend.'

Her first impression is: handsome. He's tall, lean and earthy, with a head of dusky blond hair, and dazzling blue eyes. Even his hooked nose is sexy. He's dressed in jeans, sneakers and a dark purple shirt and has a small, crooked smile on his face. He seems shy. Good, Dawn thinks, a man shouldn't be too confident and slick, that's usually a bad sign.

'I'm Jack Green,' he says. His voice is deep and smooth.

'Come on in. Kath's changing. I barged in on her unannouced.'

Jack walks in with the gait of a cowboy, small-hipped and broad-shouldered. And that hair, so thick. He looks, all in all, virile; intellectual is not the word that comes to mind. He goes directly to the couch and sits, placing his large, broad hands on his knees. Dr. Johnson springs from the floor onto his lap. He expertly rubs the sides of the cat's face, swerving his thumb around to get behind the ear.

'Do you have a cat?' Dawn asks.

He nods. 'Her name's Chop Suey. She's ginger striped.'

'So, Jack, what do you do?' She is dying to know.

He says, 'Carpenter.'

'For a living?'

'Yup.'

'You make chairs and tables and things?'

He says, 'I work in a scene shop. I build theater sets. Lotta Broadway shows have been built in our shop.'

He's in the theater. Why didn't he just say so? 'That sounds fascinating,' she says. 'Do you design at all?'

'Nah, I just build. But believe me, it's an art unto itself. We have a gigantic warehouse out in Greenpoint. Build the sets there, take them apart and ship 'em into Manhattan or wherever. Unless it's for a road show. That's a whole other ball game. Then you have to make them portable.'

'Do you live in Brooklyn, too?'

'Boerum Hill. Nice neighborhood. Not far from work.'

'So, you grew up in Brooklyn?' Dawn asks, and listens for a telltale accent.

'Scarsdale,' he says, aware that this one word tells a story of privilege.

Dawn is duly impressed and curious. A carpenter from Scarsdale is downscale upscale sorta, and that's an interesting enigma if nothing else.

'How about you?' Jack asks her.

'I'm a book editor. In fact, Kath's going to do some work for me.'

'Oh?'

'We just decided tonight.'

Kath emerges in blue jeans, red basketball sneakers and a black scoop-necked sweater. Big silver hoop earrings glint through the long blanket of thick, silky hair. Dawn notices a touch of pink lipstick.

'Well,' says Dawn, 'I have to get going.' Kath does not protest. 'Call me tomorrow at the office, when you get up.' Dawn gathers her bag from the floor and slings it over her shoulder.

Jack stands next to Kath. They make a sexy couple and Dawn can't help thinking that they would have beautiful children.

'Okay,' says Kath. 'I'll call you early.'

'Whenever you get up is fine.' Dawn starts to leave.

Kath says, 'Oh, Dawn, is that this guy's real name? *MauvaisT*

Dr. Johnson strolls to the door, purring. Dawn stoops to give him one last pet.

'His real name is Blitsky,' she says. 'Mike Blitsky.'

Three

Misled Mike Mauvais and his Marvelous Men

All Hank can think about is Dawn. He loves her. At least he thinks he does. Unless he was just using her to get back at Chris. Does he love Chris? He can't tell. If this knotted feeling in his stomach is love, then he guesses he does. However, the tight feeling could be fear, in which case he probably does not love Chris at all. There is no doubt in his mind that Dawn wants him back, not after last night. She must be waiting by the phone and pestering her secretary for messages, expecting to hear from him. Yes, he will call her later this afternoon. Maybe he'll even ask her out tonight. Maybe they could spend the night together, this time at her place — formerly, their place. His whole being warms at the thought. The two of them together in their old, comfortable digs. He painted the walls of that apartment with his own two hands, finished the floors, built the efficiency storage unit in the second closet. They could get themselves AIDS tested and have condomless sex, just like old times. He will re-propose to her. He still has the engagement ring she sent back to him. Should he give her that same ring, or get another one? Is there a sentimental value in giving the original ring, or just bad memories? He'll need a woman's advice. Maybe he could ask Carla. As for Chris, she is a burned bridge, after last night. She must be. He didn't come home, and he didn't call. And he won't call. Just thinking about her, he gets that boiling feeling. The little snit! Hairspray in his face!

He must think about work. Work before love. Real men take care of business first. He has a two o'clock meeting with

Mike Blitsky and had better firm up his game plan before sitting down to talk. Hank is always completely professional with his clients, crisp and well-prepared. No slackness allowed. After all, he is partner material, and he means to make that clear to his boss.

Mike Blitsky, a.k.a. Mike Mauvais of Misled Mike's Marvelous Men (a.k.a. Miss Mike), is a transvestite who ran a prostitution ring that employed transvestites — until he was caught. An enormous amount of publicity has already been generated over the case, and it hasn't even gone to trial. The crux of the defense, based on the assumption that no one in his right mind is going to come forward and actually admit to visiting a transvestite prostitute, will be three-fold: there is no solid proof of illegal activity, just suspicion and an arrest; Mike, a transvestite, is being exploited by the media; and, therefore, Mike, who is guilty only of moral outrageousness, has already been hung by the public and is himself the victim. In other words, just because the man's a flaming fag doesn't make him a prostitute. It has even occurred to Hank to sue the media for libel, but he's decided against it; better just concentrate on getting the poor sucker off.

Hank orders lunch from the deli downstairs (ham and swiss on wholewheat with mustard, mayonnaise and tomato, spring water and a small bag of Famous Amos chocolate chip cookies with macadamia nuts) and eats at his desk. He has barely made a dent in the cookies when three brisk knocks on his office door announce Carla.

She sticks her head into his office. 'Mr. Lowe,' she says in her most professional voice.

'Yes?'

'Mr. Blitsky is here for your two o'clock appointment.' She rolls her eyes and flares her nostils.

'Is it two o'clock already?' he says in his deep, professional tone. He quickly wipes all traces of lunch into the wastepaper basket, except for the barely touched cookies which he tosses into a drawer, brushes crumbs from his shirt, wipes his mouth with his hand and clears his throat.

'Yes, Mr. Lowe,' she says, 'it is.'

'Show Mr. Blitsky in, please, Carla.'

A short, fat man fills the lower half of Hank's doorway. Mike Blitsky, Mike Mauvais, Misled Mike, Miss Mike. The man is only five feet tall (if that) and makes up for his lack of height in width. He is both huge and tiny, with cropped black hair that stands on his head like a brush. His face is wide and round, and he has no visible neck. He's dressed in a dark suit which is crisply tailored to impress the man who is supposed to pry away the law. Conservatism, however, stops there. He's wearing makeup: rouge on his cheeks, green eye shadow, jet black eyebrows drawn above his eyes and bright fuchsia lipstick (the same color Chris wears). Then Hank notices the earrings on his right side: four tiny diamonds studding his lobe.

Hank steps around his desk and reaches toward Blitsky. They shake hands. Mike's palm feels soft and wet. To hide his discomfort, Hank stares into Mike's eyes, which are traced with black eyeliner, and smiles.

'I'm Henry Lowe. People call me Hank.'

Blitsky's smile is enormous and he has a big gap between his front teeth.

'But may I call you Hank?' he says nasally.

'Of course. Please, have a seat.'

Blitsky hikes up his pants, revealing hot-pink ankle socks, and plops himself down in the armchair opposite Hank's desk. 'Some people call me Mike,' he says. 'But please, never Mr. Blitsky.'

Hank sits behind the fortress of his desk. He feels like laughing. So this is his new client! Hank can see why the media love Mike, he's everything decent people try not to be: garish, flagrantly obscene, *arrested.* That is the issue here, not who Mike Blitsky is but what Mike Mauvais has done. He is being accused of breaking the law. Hank's job is to defend him of that accusation. Blitsky has a right to a lawyer, and obviously he has the money for a lawyer from Dick, Lesser & Moore. Hank wills himself to focus on these facts.

'I've gone over your written statement,' he says soberly. 'It's an interesting story. Now, tell me the truth.'

Mike weaves his chubby fingers together over his rotund middle. He smiles. 'You want the facts, I guess.'

'It's imperative, if you want me to help you.'

'Well, there are facts, and there are details. Juicy details, ya know what I mean? And everywhere doth the twain meet.' He chuckles. 'You've got all the facts in the statement. What the police busted was an honest to goodness escort service. We're not hookers. We're friends-for-hire, that's all. We're a for-hire service. I mean, there's for sale and *there's for sale.*' He rolls his eyeballs back until only the whites show.

Hank doesn't believe it for a minute, but he has to go with Blitsky, see where he takes him. 'So, there was no prostitution involved, at all?'

Mike's eyes roll back to normal. He stares at Hank and flutters his eyelids. In a singsong voice, he says, 'Our clients paid for an escort for the evening. Dinner and dancing. A girl to keep him company. That's all I ever arranged. If something else happened after dinner, well....' The corners of his mouth curl up. He shrugs.

'You say "girl." Were any of your escorts men?'

'Technically speaking, they all were. Technically speaking, so am I. But am I, really? In my heart and soul? A man? You tell me.'

Of course Blitsky is a man. But if Hank says so, will he insult his client? If he lies and says, No, you look like a woman to me, won't he then be playing along with this perverse little head game?

'I, uh, understand you are a male. You appear to be a male, of a sort. But, uh, somewhat effeminate, so to speak.' Why is he even answering Blitsky's question? Now he feels like the fool. Blitsky smiles. He's doing this on purpose, to intimidate him. Well, he won't let it happen. He will seize the upper hand.

'Mike, do you object to the term "transvestite"? Because it will be used to describe your escorts. Do you understand that?'

Blitsky shrugs. 'Transvestite, transhmestite. What do I care? Just keep me out of jail.'

'The tack I'm going to take,' Hank says, 'is that you're being used by the media as a clown in a morality play. That the public has already sized you up, judged you. That before the case even gets started, you are, essentially, a convicted man. Follow me?'

'I'd follow you anywhere.'

Hank is stunned, but he quickly gathers himself and continues. 'The public has been fed misconceptions about Mike Blitsky. You have been seized upon as an example of flagrant immorality. If this case comes to trial, I am going to demonstrate that morality is relative, and that the appearance of immorality is not against the law. Taking it even further, you, having been slandered by the media — they spoke for you, about you, and against you —*you* are the real victim. Mike, I think we have a chance of winning this case.'

Mike smiles, Hank nods, and for a moment they are in accord. Then Hank says, 'Tell me about your clients. Your statement alludes to well-known people, but you don't give any names.'

'Lillian Hellman,' Mike says, and sighs.

After a pause, Hank says soberly, 'Actually, she has been dead for years.'

'I feel like Lillian. Everyone wants names just like in the McCarthy days. But, you know, I really can't.'

Hank nods. 'I understand, but if you want to win this case, I'll need to know, confidentially. I'll need a trump card to stop the case from going to court if it looks like we won't win in front of a jury.'

'What would you say my chances are right now?' Mike asks.

Hank thinks for a moment, then says, 'Fifty-fifty. With the names, eighty-twenty in your favor. It's dirty poker, but sometimes you need to scare someone. Mike, who would be afraid of you?'

Finally, Mike says, 'John Hallory.'

'The actor?' Hank asks, writing the name on his pad.

'Yes. And Ahmed Khoranian.'

Hank's eyes snap to Mike's face. 'He's a top aide to the governor.'

'And Ann Lewis.'

'Senator Lewis's wife?'

'I'll have to shower all day, I feel so dirty.'

'This is absolutely confidential, you can rely on that.'

Mike half smiles. 'That's what my publisher said.'

'Publisher?'

'I'm doing a book.' Mike shrugs. 'I need the money to pay you, for one thing.'

Clearly alarmed, Hank asks, 'When are they publishing?'

'I'm not sure. Fall, I think. It seems fast but they hired a big-shot ghost writer.'

Hank shakes his head. 'Fall is too soon. We have to win the case first. Do you realize how damaging this could be? Mike, have you signed a contract yet?'

Warily, Mike answers, 'Yes.'

'How much did they pay you?' Hank scribbles notes as Mike speaks.

'A cool million,' Mike says with a big smile, but the squeak in his voice belies his nervousness. 'Is this really a problem? They promised to be discreet.'

'They don't pay that much for something discreet. Who's your publisher?'

'Weatherhoff, just across from Saks.'

'Who are you working with there?' Hank peels to a new page on his pad and keeps writing.

'Nice gal, on my wavelength, my success is her success blah blah blah.'

'Name?'

'Dawn Waterstone, I think.'

'Waterston,' Hank mutters, as his mind tunes out to and in to the difficulties this situation is bound to cause. Dawn, Mike's editor: this must be the big break she referred to last night. Last night in bed. He loves her, wants to marry her, re-engage. But pitted against each other professionally, it will never work. He adjures himself to think, be rational, make a plan, take action to resolve the dilemma. He will speak with her, she will understand, she will offer to withdraw from the project so he can move forward and really lock horns with the new editor — because she will know that he can't lock horns with her and still love her. She knows him well enough to understand that. And to know that if he has to block the book, he will. She will have to withdraw. But will she, really? She has changed somewhat, become a little tougher, more self-possessed. All of which he knows is his fault. If he had never left her, she would still be reliably pliable. Now he remembers clearly what she said, that this project was going to be a boon for her career. She's excited about it. Just like he is. He certainly can't withdraw from the case; Dick, Lesser & Moore does not retreat because of some wimpy publisher. He feels stuck, crushed between circumstance and inevitability. He must find the road to action, and take it; he must stay firmly in control.

'Earth to Hank. Earth to Hank.'

'What?'

'You still with me here?'

It's Mike, staring at Hank, snapping his fingers.

'Sorry. Okay, Mike. Everything is going to be fine. I'll talk to the publisher, see what we can do. I'll work it out somehow. One step at a time, that's the only way.'

'What now?'

'Routine. Depositions. Paperwork. It'll take a while. Just sit tight.' Hank rises and walks around his desk.

Mike gets up and they shake hands. 'Don't call me, I'll call you?' Mike singsongs.

'You can always call me,' Hank says.

Mike winks. 'That was exactly our motto at Misled Mike's.'

Hank says. 'Oh, and Mike, please get me a list of all your clients today.'

'I gave you three names.'

'Yes, but I need to see the whole picture.'

Mike hesitates. 'I have an unwritten contract with my clients. That list is confidential.'

'Former clients, Mike. Whose neck is on the block now?'

Mike nods slowly. 'Okay.'

'Messenger it to me this afternoon.'

By five o'clock, Hank has Mike's neatly typed list of one-hundred twenty-four men and three women. If it comes to it — if he finds himself racing with the book, and can just manage to get his foot forward first — Hank will hit hard and low. He'll subpoena Mike's star clients as witnesses for the defense. Once the D.A.'s office hears about that, they'll do anything to stop it. They won't let these people up on the stand as clients of transvestite prostitutes. Not a famous actor, the governor's top aide and a senator's wife. The implications of that would be far worse than letting one poor sucker loose on a mistrial. As long as the book doesn't get published before the trial and implicate Mike's clients before Hank has a chance to use them to bargain anonymity for dropping the charges against Mike. He will have to impress Mike with the absolute necessity of keeping the clients' names, or any identifying descriptions, out of the book.

Hank sits slumped in his chair, thinking, or at least attempting to stave off debilitating confusion. At about seven o'clock the sun begins to set. Through his office window, he can see the long stretch of Park Avenue, filled with traffic, all the way down to the Helmsley Palace. There's a bluish hue dotted with fuzzy red tail-lights. It looks so lonely down there, distant, unreal. He feels defeated. But he's a man, and a man does what he has to do.

He already left a message on Dawn's answering machine over an hour ago, asking her to call him at the office. He shrinks at the thought of what he is going to say to her. She won't be expecting it. When she gets his message, she'll think he's calling to ask her out. And he wants to. He wants to ask her out, to ask himself back into her life, to give her back the ring.

At five to eight, his phone rings.

'Hi.' It's Dawn. 'Was I surprised to get your message! I mean, I'm delighted, Hank, to hear from you so soon.'

'How are you?' he says. *Go on, tell her, get it over with.*

'Well,' she sounds breathless. 'I just walked home from Kath's. Guess what? She's got a boyfriend. Can you believe it? After all these years, a real boyfriend.'

'That's great. I'm happy for her.'

'So, when will I see you again?'

Hasn't she become bold in the last two months! There was a day when timid Dawn would never have asked a risky question like that. She would wait, a wilting flower, for him to initiate conversations, arguments, sex. She was so afraid of rejection. And then he rejected her. She certainly has made strides in her confidence — just so he can knock her down again.

'That's what I have to talk to you about. It's not that I don't, well, let me put it this way ... I had decided that I wanted to give us another try, if you were game.'

'Had? Past tense?'

'Yes. It's just, well, this. Mike Blitsky. I'm his defense attorney.'

'Oh. I see.'

'And you are his editor.'

Her voice fades, 'Yes, I am.'

'For a book that could destroy his legal case. So, I have a fight in front of me. I can't fight it with you if we're back together. It just won't work. So, there we are. I'm not willing to hand this case over to another attorney, and I assume you're not willing to give up the book. We both have something hanging on this, don't we? Don't we, Dawny?'

'You want to make partner.'

'And you want a bestseller with your stamp on it.'

'Yes, I do,' she says.

'So,' he says.

'There's something I'm curious about, Hank, if you don't mind my asking.'

'Fine.'

'Whatever happened with you and Chris?'

'Uh, nothing. We had a fight.'

'I heard you were living together. Not true?'

'No, true. We're living together.'

'That was present tense, Hanky.'

'Yes, I know.'

Four
Enter Marco

June 5th, the day Dawn and Hank were to marry.

Dawn has spent the whole afternoon moping around Riverside Park, ticking through the afternoon minute by minute, a time bomb of unrealized dreams. At four o'clock, a guy in leather shorts and earrings in his nose roller blades past and Dawn's body seizes up with disappointment at what would have been at this very moment, *if only.* She is in a state of retrograde wishful thinking, wishing to reverse time, to de-sequence events, to do it over but differently, better, to erase the disappointments. Four o'clock. A leader of the Ethical Culture Society would have been reading their vows to them, and they would have been answeringjw *yes I am I do I will.* A woman in layers of tattered filthy clothing pushes a shopping cart to Dawn's bench, parks it and sits down. Dawn sighs deeply and shakes her head. The woman looks at her angrily and says, 'It ain't my fault. Got any money, honey?'

Where is Hank now, at four p.m.? What is he doing? Who is he with?

Suddenly the woman is laughing. She has read Dawn's T-shirt: *If you love someone, let them go free, if they don't come back, hunt them down and kill them* stretched across her bosom like a banner of confidence. Dawn leans forward, about to rise.

The woman says, 'He's dead weight, forget him. I left in seventy-eight and only regretted it one day.' She shakes her head and her floppy knit hat bounces. Dawn thinks she sees some dust puff out. She stands, and the woman slaps her knee. 'One dollar, lady, please, please.'

Dawn digs into the pocket of her cut-offs and withdraws a clump of singles, maybe three or four, she isn't sure. She hands them to the woman and leaves.

She walks through the park to the Eighty-third Street exit. It is a spectacular day — blue sky, leafy trees swishing in a warm breeze — perfect weather for a wedding. She bursts into tears and heads home in a jog. How could that peon Blitsky have come between them so thoroughly? How could Hank have been such a heartless careerist to let it happen? Was he right in assuming that she would rather have a promotion than have him back in her life, her heart, her bed? He didn't even give her the option of participating in the decision, he simply told her his. Maybe she never even had a chance, maybe their single night of love-making was, for him, a mistake. According to Andy Shoemaker — that rich tub o'lard who's been calling her up and asking her out — Hank is back with Chris the Bitch, Manipulator of Men, Enemy of Women.

By the time Dawn reaches her building, she has convinced herself again that it's hopeless, that she must move on, find someone new. She decides, after long uncertainty, that she will go to the party Kath invited her to, at the home of some friend of Jack's. She'd really rather stay home, watch TV and eat Chinese food followed by a pint of Ben & Jerry's Chunky Monkey ice cream. She'd rather Be Here Now: depressed, lonely, fully immersed in the cruel reality of her life. Life without Hank. But she knows she will most probably never meet someone if she sequesters herself in a pod of misery. So she heads for the closet to find something to wear.

Luckily, one thing Dawn does have is clothes; her tendency to buy things just-in-case keeps her prepared. For tonight, she selects a strapless black dress that hugs her body to the hips, where it flares out in folds of transparent white-on-black polka-dotted chiffon. She also has the matching chiffon jacket and together the set makes a sexy, witty, fun dress. Dawn is none of these things; therefore she will have to portray them. The outfit will help.

She fusses around the apartment until it's time to go. She is compulsive in her cleanliness, there is no clutter. The living room is furnished with a pastel floral couch with delicately rounded corners and a frill around the bottom edge, a sparkling, glass coffee table, two white upholstered chairs angled symmetrically across from the couch for easy conversation — though, admittedly, Dawn is alone most of the time. White lace curtains, with not a shadow of a stain on them, hang sumptuously over the two windows. A large yellow and pink flowered cotton throw-rug separates the living and dining areas of the main room. The dining-table, rarely used, is round, surrounded by four Shaker chairs. In the center of the table is a thick glass vase weighted with clear glass marbles hugging the stems of four red tulips.

She takes a cab across town to an over-priced Second Avenue hirise called the Norwegian Palace, and rides the mirrored elevator to the twenty-third floor. No sooner has she rung the bell than a young man appears at the door. He isn't exactly handsome — average height, average weight, brown hair, brown eyes — but he has charm. She feels like she has seen him somewhere before.

'Hi, I'm David,' he says. 'Welcome to my home.'

Now she remembers: he plays a young husband in a series of detergent ads. He and his trim young wife would be jogging along a suburban street, when suddenly he would trip into a mud puddle. Or they would be sitting on the living room couch in candlelight, drinking red wine, and his passionate lunge would douse her silky white negligee. Or he would come breathlessly into the laundry room, where she would be standing — waiting? — with ketchup and mustard and chocolate sauce on his shirt, which she would promptly strip off and magnify for the viewing audience before tossing it into the washing machine. No matter what the scenario, they always ended up in the laundry room, clean and kissing.

Dawn introduces herself and promptly sheds her chiffon jacket to reveal her nicely formed shoulders. You never know. This David, this familiar face from the tube, could be her new Lover.

'It's so nice to meet you,' Dawn says, smiling. 'Jack's told me so much about your budding career.' A lie.

'Really?' David smiles. Something about his perfect teeth tells Dawn, suddenly, that she will never be able to love this man.

'Guess I'll mingle,' she says, and moves along.

The walls of David's studio apartment are white, the furniture is black, and one expensive chrome-plated hallo-gen lamp swoops up from the floor to a curved height of seven feet. It looks like a big, old-fashioned hair drier, servicing the wall-to-wall heads. Dawn gets a drink from the bar — a one-by-one foot counter space in the closet-sized kitchen — and stands demurely in a corner, desperately searching for Kath and Jack, even more desperately trying to hide her discomfort. Where are they? Probably lounging around together, having a great time. Kath should have warned her; she wouldn't have come. Which is why, of course, Kath did *not* warn her. Who are all these people? She feels deeply uncomfortable. Does it show?

A short, compact man with jet black hair and big brown eyes stops in front of her and nods. He's kind of cute. What the hell. Dawn smiles.

'You look uncomfortable,' he says to her.

Dawn shrugs her bare shoulders. 'There's been a death in my family,' she lies. 'I'm just getting over it.'

'Someone close?'

'A distant cousin. But still a shock.'

'I'm sorry. Freshen your drink?'

'Okay. Red wine. Thanks.' She hands him her glass. He returns immediately.

'Marco Bobst,' he says, extending a hand.

Dawn likes the warm, dry feel of his hand as they shake. It feels like a doctor's hand. Could he be her future husband?

'Dawn Waterston,' she says.

Marco's smile reveals straight teeth with a slight gap between the upper front two. His thick black eyebrows connect at the top of his nose.

He places a hand firmly against her back and leads her to the corner of the studio, where two couples dance to a loud Fine Young Canibals song. Marco starts to move. He's sexy, and Dawn feels her body heat up. Her mind calculates. Maybe if she drinks enough, she'll go home with him, or bring him to her place. She's got the condoms in her purse.

He pulls her to him and sways his hips gently against hers. Now fear creeps in: The New Reality: Fear of AIDS. Cool down, Dawny, she tells herself, everything is going to be okay. You're meeting new men, that's natural, go with it, but slowly slowly slowly.

Marco's thick meaty shoulder protruding from the green and pink striped sheet annoys Dawn. This reminds her of the old days of promiscuity, pre-AIDS. In retrospect, she hated sleeping around, but only realized it when she met Hank and their domestic bliss was paramount. She has a nagging feeling that she recognizes Marco. Then it hits her — he reminds her of Mike Blitsky — and the connection propels her out of bed.

Suddenly she is aware that she can't remember exactly what happened last night. She knows she drank too much at the party, and then .... How did they end up back here? Presumably they had sex. Did she enjoy it? *Did they use a condom?* She looks around for evidence and sees none. Anxiety ruptures in her chest as the potential significance of this transgression sinks in.

As she clumsily wraps herself in her silk kimono (a gift from Hank, on the first anniversary of their meeting), Marco turns over and stretches both arms to the ceiling with an enormous yawn.

'Hi,' he says in a gravelly morning voice.

He looks sweet and boyish with his rumpled black hair and sleepy eyes. She smiles, despite herself. She can't help noticing, in the early morning sunshine, that Marco's arms are particularly muscular. He flings the sheet away from his body and she can see that he is in excellent shape. Her eyes light on a crumpled, deflated rubber stuck to the sheet near his leg, and relief— almost joy — courses through her.

She smiles, and asks, 'Do you work out?'

'I lift weights.'

'Well,' she says, 'it shows.' She stands there for a moment and looks at him. She feels trapped in her own apartment with a stranger, and worse, one with whom she has evidently copulated. Still, she invited him here — at least she assumes she did — and as she has always prided herself on being a generous hostess, asks: 'Coffee? Bagels? Sunday *Times?*'

Marco says, 'Thanks, great,' and Dawn departs to the kitchen feeling like a hostage bent on good behavior.

She arranges a nice breakfast at the ne'er used dining-table: delicately hand-painted ceramic plates, matching mugs, sky blue cloth napkins, three chunky bagels hastily defrosted in the microwave, sweet butter, cream cheese, jam, orange juice. Hank's heart would melt. But he isn't here. Composing herself, she calls, 'Breakfast is ready!'

Marco emerges in black bikini underpants, his inert penis noticeably squeezed in.

'Wow,' he says. 'Nice spread.'

'Thank you,' Dawn says. 'I like to make Sunday mornings special.' A lie. She usually eats a bagel with cream cheese straight off the wax paper from the store, while hunched over the newspaper, poppyseeds falling with every bite, her hair a total mess, her mind a groggy blank.

She pours coffee, they eat and share the *Times.* After a while, she asks, 'So, what do you do?'

He looks up and coolly answers, 'I work in international banking.'

'Really?' Dawn finds herself suddenly interested. Now she wants the whole story: place of residence, of birth, education, income, benefits. She says, 'How fascinating. Tell me more.'

Marco smiles and delves happily into his personal resume. 'Well, I live downtown in a loft, co-op, bought it last year. Grew up here in the city, high school at Dalton, B.A. at Cornell, M.B.A. at Columbia, straight into a management program at the bank, and here I am now. Not a unique scenario, but not a bad one, either — I like to think.'

Dawn nods, and says, 'I like to think, too.'

'No, I mean I like to think I had a good start in life. That's what I meant, not that I like to *think.*'

'Oh, sorry.'

'I'm secure now,' he continues. 'I'm ready, you know?'

Carefully, Dawn asks, 'Ready for what?'

'You know,' he says, 'marriage.'

Bingo. Following some compulsory dating, Marco has the keys to her apartment. Dawn feels a bit stunned by this sudden turn of events, but also excited, hopeful, wishful. To hell with love, she thinks, deciding that for once she will attempt to engineer her personal life, create it, use her mind.

But something is missing; as time passes, she becomes aware that it just doesn't feel right, that in truth, she is still in love with Hank. She develops a notion that if news of her affair with Marco spreads to Hank, he'll come back to claim her. So she decides to throw a little dinner party, just a small gathering for a few close friends. She invites Kath and Jack, Janice from work, and Andy Shoemaker. Her plan is for Andy to leak word of Marco to Hank. The domino effect. The ripple will come back to her, if she's lucky, in the form of a jealous Hank. Yet even as she makes these plans, she denies her true intentions, refusing to believe herself capable of such overt manipulations, and also preparing herself for disappointment. She has acted before on the fires of wishful thinking, a pattern her former therapist perceived, which Dawn then described to Kath, and which her friend will apparently never let her forget.

Meanwhile, she continues to spend time with Marco, and inconsistencies begin to surface. Such as, when she tries to reach him at his home number, on the nights he isn't with her, she always gets his answering service. But she can reliably reach him at work; he can be counted on to answer his own phone 'Marco Bobst!' with authority. Then, on the evening of the dinner party, a Friday, Marco tells her he is going home after work to change his clothes, wishing to be more casually dressed for the dinner than in his conservative banker's suit. When she needs a few shallots from the Korean market on the corner and a bottle of white wine, and doesn't have time to run out for them herself, she calls and calls his home number but the service always answers.

She hears his keys jangle in the lock at precisely seven-thirty, as promised, and rushes to the front door. He is wearing khaki pants, a denim shirt and a tweed jacket.

'Where were you?' she asks.

'Home,' he says. 'I went home to change.' He kisses her tenderly on the lips.

She pulls away. 'I tried to call. Why does your service always answer?'

'Oh, sorry. I do that to avoid business calls at home. I just didn't check the service tonight. Did you need something?'

'I already went out myself. Now I'm running late.' The proverbial nail hammered in, she ignores him and returns to her preparations.

Janice arrives first. Also an editor at Weatherhoff, they've known each other for three years and have worked their way up the ranks together. They rarely see each other out of the office, but thinking that Janice and Andy might hit if off, Dawn invited her. Janice enters cheerfully, with an offering of pastries from Balduccis. She's short and slightly plump, and dresses without flair. But what she lacks in style, she makes up for in kindness and real estate. She lives in a rent-controlled one-bedroom in Greenwich Village. Based on the belief that there is someone for everyone, Dawn is confident that one day, some nice guy will fall in love with Janice and move in. Who knows, maybe Andy? He could certainly use a new locale.

By eight-fifteen, no one else has arrived and Dawn feels the adreneline pumping in her chest, about to accelerate into hysteria. She sits with Marco and Janice, feigning nonchalance, sipping wine, picking at the hors d'oeurves: flatbread with brie and capers, humus and carrot sticks, a substantial chunk of Vermont cheddar surrounded by saltless cream wafers. Janice, who occupies one of the armchairs, talks about things at work. It's dull, but it passes the time.

At eight-twenty, the phone rings.

Dawn answers, 'Hello!'

It's Andy Shoemaker, canceling, explaining that he has to work late. Thus dissolves Dawn's *modus operandi* for this dinner party. But she can't let on; it would be far too embarrassing. She politely releases Andy from the guilt-hook, and casually agrees to let him take her out to dinner 'to make up for tonight,' as he said.

Dawn wishes Marco and Janice would just leave — together, if necessary. Just as she is spiraling down toward depression, the doorbell rings, and she ushers in Kath and Jack.

'Sorry we're late,' she says, kissing Dawn on the cheek. Dawn tensely accepts their greetings, and pulls back quickly to shine at them with hostess-cheer.

Kath reads her instantly, and asks, 'You okay?'

'Fine. Andy just canceled.'

'More food to go around,' Jack says, verring toward the hors d'oeurves.

Kath maneuvers Dawn to the kitchen, and demands, 'What's wrong?'

Dawn sighs, shakes her head, and cannot find words to describe her disappointment.

'So that's the guy, huh?' Kath asks softly. 'Your new boyfriend.'

Dawn nods.

Kath hesitates. 'He seems nice.'

'I miss Hank,' Dawn says.

Kath puts an arm around Dawn's shoulders. 'I know you do. Just give it time.'

Five
Love Bites Back

O! misery. Hank is doomed — doomed to unhappiness. Life with Chris is a cycle of screaming jags and hot sex. And she's expensive. Despite the fact that she holds down a decent job, Hank is required to pay the rent, the utilities, for groceries (which he has to get himself), to do all the household chores, and to buy love-gifts such as jewelry and lingerie. Chris swears she has no money.

'Where does it go?' Hank mourns of her salary.

And she tells him, point blank, like a bullet to his head: 'Clothes.'

The night he returned — after that sweet bout of love with Dawn — his first step back into life with Chris was right into a pizza. It was bad enough returning to their cramped apartment, but what he found to greet him was a greasy pizza box on the hall floor, with half a cold pie inside, into which his good shoe landed immediately over the threshold. Pepperoni with extra cheese, Chris's favorite. She, meanwhile, sat on the couch watching a rerun of 'Dynasty' (Die Nasty) on TV, and when Hank cried out, notifying her of his return, her response was a strident 'Shh!'

That's when he noticed she had red hair. Yesterday morning, it was blond.

'Your hair,' he murmured.

'Your shoe,' she laughed.

And so resumed their domestic life.

Hank doesn't know what to do. He loves Dawn. But he's living with Chris. It must be unfair to hate the woman you live with. Disturbed by the notion that he is far more emotionally dysfunctional than he had realized, he considers whether he is a classic woman hater, and can only be content when miserable. But if he hated women, wouldn't the elixir be *their* misery? Perhaps, then, the problem is one of self esteem; that his measure of happiness is how badly someone else treats him. He buys *Men Who Hate Women and The Women Who Love Them, Iron John* and *Creative Visualization,* locks them in a desk drawer at work and reads a page or two when he can.

As for his night-long disappearance, Chris says nothing, which scares him more than anything. She's cool and collected, and it drives him crazy with uncertainty. He came back of his own free will, and knows that he must take responsibility for this; that if he stays, he must stay wholeheartedly, and if he leaves he should leave fast and clean. As he considers leaving her, he finds to his surprise that his ambivalence runs deep. He has strong feelings for her, but they are very mixed: love and hate, lust and disgust. He felt ambivalent when he walked out on Dawn, and now he's the picture of regret. He can't help wondering whether, if he leaves Chris, he'll end up just as guilty and regretful. So, he decides not to decide, and consoles himself with the thought that when the right solution presents itself, he will act on it.

Meanwhile, he works late most nights, building Blitsky's case, haggling with editor Dawn over the phone. When he hears her voice, he feels those butterflies tumbling in his stomach. O! lost. A man on the spiritual skids.

One night, when Hank gets home from work, late as usual, he finds Chris sitting at the dining room table as if in thought. This strikes him as very strange. Normally she is either eating, talking, sleeping, working, getting dressed or undressed, or watching TV. He has never seen her just sit there.

'What's wrong?' he asks.

A pink headband pushes her red hair away from her face. She's wearing pink hot pants and a tie-died, skin-tight T-shirt.

She just sits there, an assault of color and sexuality, and stares at him.

'What did I do?' he asks.

And finally she says, 'Where were you that night?'

'What night?'

'The night you didn't come home.'

'I told you I wasn't coming home.'

'You did not.'

'I did. Maybe you didn't hear — the elevator doors were shut — but I told you.'

'So where were you?'

'I stayed at Andy's.'

She says, 'I slept with Andy once.' Then, 'Don't worry. It was before I met you. Anyway, he doesn't really get hard.'

Hank feels his face tighten and his stomach lurch. Angry remarks spring to mind. Who is he madder at: Andy for the deception, or Chris for the shock? But Hank says nothing. What can he say? He slept with Dawn the night he left Chris. Better just to avoid the topic completely.

'So? What do you say to that, Hank?'

He sighs. 'Why are you telling me this now?'

'Because.'

'Look, Chris, either tell me or leave me alone.'

'Andy called me today.'

Hank is silent, terrified, and waits for the verdict of what Andy might have revealed.

'He told me you brought a woman to his place the night you stayed there.'

'He told you that?' Hank says, trying to sound incredulous.

'Yes, he told me that! Who was it?'

'You're jumping to conclusions. What makes you think Andy was telling the truth?'

Outsmart her. It's his word against Andy's, after all.

'I knew you'd been with someone, I just didn't know who. Don't even try to bluff your way out of this. Just goddamn tell me!' Her hand comes slamming down on the table and two brass candlesticks totter noisily.

Hank, a grown, mature, possibly brilliant man, becomes a puddle of fear. 'Listen, Chris, honey,' he says sweetly. 'I, uh, well, I don't know what to say. You know I love you —'

'Bullshit!' And the hand slams down again. And the candlesticks shake. And Hank turns to pure liquid. 'Who?'

'It was ... it was ... it was just someone I met. It was nothing. *Really.*'

Does she know it was Dawn? Did Andy tell her?

'Oh yeah?'

'Yes, yes!' His mind reels: compose yourself, do not allow this woman to control you, keep the reins, set the rules, be a man! 'It was just a girl I met at a bar. It meant nothing. Are you happy now?'

She says, 'And I suppose now we both have AIDS!'

'I used a condom, rest assured of that.'

If Hank were lucky, Chris would pack her bags and leave him. But he is not lucky, he is decidedly unlucky.

'Uh huh. Yup. Sure.' She leans forward and tells him, in a low but commanding voice: 'Now listen to me, Henry Lowe, here's how it's gonna hang from now on. First, we're gonna go get ourselves AIDS tested. Second, we're gonna get serious. You're gonna marry me.'

Which is how Chris comes to acquire Dawn's engagement ring. Afterwards, Hank cannot help but wonder why he gave her the ring. Why did he let her control him? Why didn't he just leave? Well, he reassures himself, he's no fool; he could see the noose tightening as he tried to wriggle away. To all appearances, he lost his courage, became powerless, couldn't make a decision and simply obeyed. But he knows, deep down — at least he hopes — that he will extricate himself from this situation with Chris, as soon as the solution presents itself.

Later, after feeding Hank leftover Chinese food for dinner and making him do the dishes, Chris says, 'I lied to you about Andy. I slept with him twice.'

Hank asks, 'When?'

'I'll tell you when you tell me who you really spent that night with. But anyway, the rest was true. Andy's hard-ons stink.'

Six

The Truth is Better than Nothing

Dawn barrels up Madison Avenue in her purple linen mini-dress, white stockings and battered sneakers. Needles of bright summer sunshine flick off the long gold earrings (gift from Hank, no occasion) that dangle and swing by her neck. She uses her brown leather briefcase as both a shield and a weapon.

Red alert!

A handsome young man in a suit is walking right toward her. He looks like Hank. Her eyes flash to his left hand, zoom in on his fourth finger. No ring. In five seconds, Dawn meets, dates, beds, marries, and divorces him. The bastard. As he passes her, she swipes him with the corner of her briefcase. He looks at her in shock. She clamps her lips, raises her chin and marches on.

Men!

By the time she gets to the lobby of her office building, rage has exhausted her. O! life. In this river of humanity she is but a minor speck. What does it all mean? Why get up in the morning? Why go to work at all? Why read the newspaper? she thinks as she drops coins into the hand of the man in the lobby news kiosk. Every day, the same routine. He even knows her name though she has forgotten his.

He says, 'Yo, Dawn, on the rag or something?'

In a split second, she manages to glare at him so profoundly as to considerably darken his morning. She says, 'Thank you,' coolly, and progresses to the elevator bank.

On the rag or something. Okay, all right, so she is about to get her period, so she is a little tense, so she is about to murder the first person who rubs her the wrong way. Watch out, iron men: full moon alert, females in rage!

On the way up in the elevator, Dawn closes her eyes, takes three deep breaths and puts a smile on her face. She concentrates on exuding calmness, poise, professionalism as she walks down the hall to her office. Tony is already at his desk, dependable as always. He's a young Asian man with literary aspirations who supposes Dawn doesn't know he is writing a novel on the hard disk. The moment he senses her approach, he slaps keys and the screen flashes blank blue then suddenly a boilerplate memo format is there. She doesn't care; he's the best assistant in the department and she knows she's lucky to have him. Tony, typing his renown hundred-words-per-minute, instantly creates a memo as Dawn walks up behind him.

'Good morning,' he says.

She tries to smile and says, 'Morning.'

He looks alarmed. 'What's wrong?'

'I'm on the rag!' she shouts and slams her office door.

Somehow, Tony manages to keep people away from her all morning. He's amazing, really: pleasant, organized, friendly, competent and willing to do anything to help her. Once, early on, she caught him sharpening her pencils with a look of suppressed misery on his face, and she felt downright evil. Recalling how during her own apprenticeship such extremely menial tasks had had the power to demean and humiliate her beyond justification, she decided instantly that she would teach her staff dignity. Staff; well, Tony. Big people can fetch their own coffee and sharpen their own pencil tips, she taught him. Since that day, their professional relationship has flourished; in exchange for dignity, he has given her increasing loyalty.

Dawn's office is orderly and bright, a big window behind her desk lets in lots of sun. There is one wall of shelves on which books are neatly crammed. Her desk is covered with stacks of papers with a post-it note on top of each, reminding her what to do next. If she doesn't straighten up her work-clutter at the end of each day, and leave herself these little reminders, she won't have the faintest idea what to do the next morning. Everyone applauds her organization, but Dawn secretly worries about a failing memory. And today she is concerned about her sanity. Her old therapist told her that her feelings, when she was premenstrual, were real but accentuated. Though at times like now, when she actually feels crazy, it is hard to accept that this delerium of intense emotion is just her real self surfacing — nothing to worry about. It worries her, a lot.

She sits in her chair and stares at the telephone. Marco. Call Marco. It's the first thing that comes to her mind — her real mind speaking to her from deep within the cloister of her inner self. She dials his office number, and a girl answers the phone, 'Word Processing.'

'I was trying to reach Marco Bobst, I must have dialed the wrong extension.'

'Marco Bobst?' the girl says. 'You mean Mark. Mark got let go last week.'

'Excuse me, I don't understand.'

The girl says. 'Personnel said Word Processing had to cut back on temps and hire someone permanent. He wasn't the fastest typist, anyway.'

'Excuse me,' Dawn says, 'but what company is this?'

'World Bank New York.'

Marco did say he was 'in international banking.'

According to Dawn's calendar, the menstrual bomb should drop some time in the next twenty-four hours. Better leave Marco alone, she tells herself, and let the hormonal blitz come and go; just keep calm and wait. After all, maybe there's an explanation for all this.

She closes her eyes and takes seven deep breaths. Then, despite her better judgment, something inside her mind — a small but loud and very real maniacal voice — prompts her to dial Marco's home number. The service answers and it sounds just like Marco's voice that says, '4924.'

She knows she shouldn't — she knows she should be calm, cool and collected, fair, understanding, even forgiving— but she can't help it. Dawn shouts into the phone, 'Is this Mark Bobst, the temp?'

Silence.

'Well?'

'Dawn?'

'You bet it's Dawn.'

'I want to explain.'

She slams down the phone.

And then, before her hand has even released its insane grip on the receiver, the phone rings again. She answers. 'Dawn Waterston!'

'Dawn? Am I calling at a bad time?'

'Hank? Do you have any idea what it feels like to be me, living my life? Do you?'

There is a pause, then Hank asks, 'Have you been eating salty foods?' He used to monitor her intake of salty foods and sweets for a week before her period and record her menstrual cycle in his calendar. He said this was easier than taking the extreme abuse heaped upon him due to the retention of fluids in conjunction with wild hormonal swings.

Dawn hangs up. She dials Kath, who as usual isn't home — probably out at the library, or in Bayonne researching Blitsky.

Dawn's mood sinks lower and lower. She waits out the morning, then feigns illness and goes home. She puts on her cut-offs and a T-shirt and takes a long, sullen walk in Central Park. While there, she buys and eats: one souvlaki, one bag of salted popcorn, one diet soda, one bag of sugar-roasted pea-nuts, and an ice cream bar.

And that is just the beginning.

By nightfall, which comes at about eight-thirty, she is sitting on her bed, wearing only the T-shirt (the shorts suddenly got too tight), watching a rerun of 'Hill Street Blues' on TV in dazed incomprehension, halfway through a large bag of *Smartfood,* as if it will really help.

Enter Marco — or Mark — with his own keys.

Dawn is so far gone she doesn't even care. She just sits there munching on the salty cheesy popcorn, glued to the boob tube. This is how Marco finds her. Finally, at a commercial break, she turns to look at him. He is standing in the bedroom door, staring at her.

'Don't do this to yourself,' he says with what sounds like sincerity. But how can she trust that he means what he says? After all, hasn't he told her some real, whopping lies?

'I'm not doing it to myself,' she says, 'I'm doing it to you.'

'Listen, Dawn, I'm sorry. I —'

'Just tell me,' she says sharply. 'Who are you?'

Marco's black hair shines in the blue light of the TV. He looks sad, standing alone in the doorway, in his tweed jacket, sneakers and jeans. Mark. A stranger. Where is Marco? Isn't he in there, somewhere?

'I don't know,' he says.

'I haven't been sleeping with an "I don't know." I've been sleeping with a real live person. Who? Who have I been sleeping with? What else about you is a lie? Tell me!'

'Mark Bobst,' he mumbles. 'I type.'

'And not very well, I hear.'

Marco winces.

'Sorry,' Dawn says. She pats the bed and he sits next to her. 'I don't feel well at all,' she says, and hands him the bag of popcorn. He puts it on the night table.

'I'm really sorry, Dawn,' he says. 'I just don't like myself very much, I guess. The truth is, I grew up in Brooklyn, never went to college, and live in New Jersey. That's me. Take it or leave it.'

Dawn shrugs. She is so depressed, she hardly cares at this point. 'Oh, big deal,' she says. 'I guess I'll take it.'

Marco smiles. 'You're the most understanding woman I've ever known. You're a jewel. I love you.'

He loves her. Normally, she would take this as a compliment, but somehow, given the current state of affairs, it barely lifts her heart.

He adds, 'If you don't mind, though, would you still call me Marco?'

Her mind fills suddenly with chaos, undefined conflicting reactions, and she says, quietly, 'Okay.'

The truth will set you free, but first it will destroy you — that is what they say. Dawn feels that anything is better than nothing and opts to keep Marco. She doubts she'll ever marry him, and does away with niceties such as Sunday brunch and decent meals on weeknights. Now, they eat Chinese take-out on her bed and watch TV together. It's a being alone-with-someone-else kind of togetherness. Maybe the truth will free them, eventually, to part ways; but for the time being it has locked them in automatic drive. They develop habits, and do away with joy.

Then, one hot night, they go to a party at the home of someone they have never met before, a friend of a former co-worker of Marco's. The hostess, Lacy, is blond and permed, comfortably lukewarm and very rich. She lives alone in a large one-bedroom apartment on Irving Place, a co-op purchased by her cattle-rancher father from Texas as a gift for her college graduation. Lacy is about twenty-three, Dawn would guess, and neither beautiful nor remarkably bright. Her impact lies in the general sensation she exudes of expected and received privilege, in the clarity of her skin, the sheen of her hair, the quality of her clothes, the sturdy comfort of her apartment. It strikes Dawn as odd that someone so young would have such a settled home, and that all the young friends filling it up tonight would be so wholesome and righteous and well-dressed. She feels alone in this room, longing suddenly for the old days, when exuberant unisexism precluded makeup and everyone wore Levis and plain T-shirts and when you could make love and not catch evil diseases, and when you could smoke a joint and not be immediately enrolled in a twelve-step program. She yearns for the Moody Blues, not Madonna. She yearns for the days when people were afraid that computers would rule the world.

She goes to the table where a bar has been arranged, and decides she'll have vodka tonight, even though she rarely touches anything stronger than wine.

Dawn feels that coming to this party was a mistake, and her urge is to leave. Marco, though, happily integrates into the young crowd. So she tries to engage in conversation with a young woman fresh from Smith College, wearing a black Chanel dress and a cluster of oversized crystals around her neck. The girl wants to understand the environment better, she says, to participate in its rebirth, and thus has recently returned from a hike in Utah. She is thinking of visiting the rainforest with a choral group from school. Dawn wants to barf. Instead, she says that she herself has not had much chance to travel as she has spent the last decade of her life building a career. 'That's too bad,' the girl says, vaguely, twirling her crystals. Dawn wants to leave, this is not her milieu, kids with grown-up bodies and enough money to delude themselves that singing hymns to a bunch of Brazil nuts will actually help the world. She has become so used to her own particular rut that the thought of doing anything other than grinding herself through the corporate structure, and engineering her personal time with the help of VCR, microwave and redial, seems outlandish. She remains convinced that Haagan-Dazs is a place in Sweden. No, Dawn does not like this room full of young retrograde hipster environmentalists, and finds herself gazing into the crowded party thinking how shocked they'll all be when reality hits them, too. She retreats to silence, and the girl gazes at her face; probably, Dawn thinks, counting wrinkles.

What finally piques her interest is the sight of Marco, across the room, talking with Lacy. He stands very close to her, leaning slightly forward, smiling with the slight, seductive curl of his lip that he used the night he seduced Dawn. His dark eyes are focused right on Lacy's pale ones, and Dawn's impulse is to laser-beam herself between them. Even if she doesn't love him, she reasons, he is still hers. But she doesn't move; she swigs the rest of her vodka and decides to have another drink even though she knows she is already beyond her limit.

The next thing Dawn knows, she is deep in an armchair, alone in a dark, unfamiliar room. She feels that awful desperate disorientation when you don't know where you are, or even exactly who you are. She becomes overwhelmed with panic, jumps to her feet and paces until, finally, she recognizes the velvet upholstery of Lacy's couch.

She locates her purse next to the couch and tiptoes out, annoyed that Marco left her here, too hungover to feel angry. She takes a taxi home, expecting to find him in bed, and deciding that tomorrow she will decide what to do about his behavior tonight.

But Marco is not there. Nor is he reachable through the answering service. Dawn leaves approximately ten messages over the course of the next two days and gets no reply.

Finally he calls and requests that they meet for lunch. Dawn knows that an invitation to lunch by a lover who has been inexplicably absent, is a euphemism for *this is the end.* She knows it was never right with Marco, and doesn't really mind ending it, and so agrees to meet him because she needs closure, but still, she wishes she had been the one to make the first move.

At one o'clock, Dawn goes to the designated Beansprout Health Bar, takes a table and waits. Marco strolls in, fifteen minutes late, wearing a dark blue suit and pale yellow tie and swinging his briefcase (which is probably empty) by his leg. Dawn shakes her head in sarcastic disbelief. Marco sees this, and responds by tightening his lips and flaring his nostrils and sitting down across from her and saying, 'Thanks for coming,' as if she were the one who just walked in late.

She stares at him. They haven't seen each other since the cattle rustler's daughter's party. Without exactly meaning to, Dawn goes, 'Mooooo.'

'I came here to talk to you,' Marco says. His voice sounds tough, he's mad. 'But what's the point? You think you've got me all figured out. You know, you're a real bitch, Dawn.'

'Excuse me? Am I the one who disappeared and left me alone at a party?'

'I didn't disappear,' he says.

'Then where were you?'

Dawn doesn't know it yet, but she would have been better off avoiding that question, on the assumption that sometimes it is better not to poison your mind with details which will only haunt you in the end.

'I was right there, in the bedroom.'

Dawn is shocked; it had not occurred to her that, as she slept in Lacy's living room, Marco was in the bedroom with the hostess.

She does not want the conversation to end here; she desperately wants the last word. So, for lack of something better, she says, 'Do you really think I didn't know that?'

'You don't know everything, you know.'

'But I know more than enough.'

'You only know what you think you know.'

He wants the last word, too. It's a useless battle, former lovers witlessly trying to out-talk each other. 'At least I know the truth,' Dawn says. 'Oh sure, you know the truth about everything.' 'No. I only know the truth about you. You slimebag!' And with that, because she knows by now that this ridiculous conversation will go on forever unless she takes some action, she grabs her purse and stalks dramatically out of the luncheonette.

Seven
In Love and in Luck

Bayonne on a hot June morning. Kath has been here twice already, attempting to dig up information about Mike Blitsky a.k.a. Mauvais. Although she hasn't come up with anything yet, at least the hours she has put in are paid time. In any event, she likes doing research, and this Blitsky thing is intriguing in a scandalous kind of way.

Information about his real life — whoever he started as, whoever is still there buried under layers of persona — is less accessible than for the average person who lives from point to point, leaving trails in straight lines. The history of Mike Blitsky is a spiral; finding its thread is a challenge and following it will be an adventure. She has studied the publicity photo that Dawn gave her: Mike sits in a chair, looking straight into the camera with his shrewd eyes topped by drawn-on eyebrows, smiling fully, lips painted red, face large and round. He is a short, fat man trying to look like a demure woman; and with his sheer unselfcon-sciousness, his sense that he is truly sexy, he partly succeeds.

She likes that in him, his love of himself. She also likes the stories Dawn tells her about his outrageousness. Kath feels truly curious as she looks for his past; she wants to know where he came from, where his bawdy amorality originated, and how this twentieth century man could so approximate in spirit a character that would more comfortably belong to her eighteenth century studies. Until now, until loving Jack changed things, the fictions of that bygone time and the lives of those who made them, had been rich enough in imagination to content her. Nothing had fascinated her quite like BoswelPs *Life of Johnson,* or Sterne's *Tristam Shandy* with his illustrious nose and endless moment of birth. Nothing had thrilled her like Clarissa's unrequited love and those hundreds of pages of unspent passion. None of Kath's occasional lovers over the years had ever touched her as deeply as that, until Jack. It doesn't make sense, particularly, which she feels is half the beauty of it.

Blitsky wasn't born in Bayonne, that she knows from searching birth records. And since there are no records of his driver's license in the town hall, she figures — assuming he was ever here at all — that he didn't stay long enough after high school to get one, or that he doesn't drive. Can she even assume that Mike Blitsky is his real name?

Armed with the publicity shot, she goes to the public elementary school to search class photos as a last resort.

The cavernous public school appears deserted, manned by a skeletal summer staff. The green linoleum hall floors shine to a dazzle, and her sneakers squeek noisily as she walks to the head office. She finds the dark wooden door on whose milky glass *Principal* is etched in plain black lettering.

A woman in a pale yellow dress, with silvery blue-tinted curls tight on her head and bifocals perched midway along her nose, sits at a heavy wooden desk immersed in a romance novel. When Kath asks if there is. an archive of old school records, the woman stares at her for a moment above the book-jacket's enflamed, cartoony lovers, then says, 'Well, we have every file, dating back to the very beginning, if that's what you mean.'

Kath says, 'Yes. And pictures of the kids, if there are any.'

'What are you looking for, could I ask?' The woman is clearly suspicious.

Kath answers with the first thing that comes to mind, suspecting that Mike Blitsky might be a student whom any school district would prefer to forget. 'My brother,' she says.'We're putting a photo collage together for his fortieth birthday, and I'm looking for old class photos. He'll be so surprised.'

The woman perks up. 'What a nice thing to do! Here.' She lays her book down on the oaktag desk blotter and swivels around. From a bookcase behind her desk, she takes down a thick binder. 'You'll find class photos in here from the fifties and some from the sixties. It isn't a complete record, but if it was saved, it'll be in this book. Good luck.'

Kath takes the binder, thanks her and sits on a chair in the waiting area. She studies page after page of neatly arranged wallet-sized photos of geeky awkward faces with brushcuts and big ears and crooked teeth. But search as she does, no gap-toothed, large-faced, beady-eyed boy surfaces. No little Mike.

She thanks the secretary and asks where she can get a cup of coffee. The woman directs her to the lunch room down the hall, saying, 'You may find Hilda in,' punctuated by a small, sharp laugh.

Kath listens to her footsteps squeegee on the polished floor as she walks down the long, wide hall. As soon as she passes through the door into the empty cafeteria, she hears a faint sound of singing. It gets louder as she approaches an-other door, which leads her into an industrial kitchen. A hefty woman in an orange and pink flowered moomoo stands at a counter, singing 'My Way' and slicing a flat cake layer with a very large knife. She has wiry grey hair and wears round glasses.

Kath takes a couple of steps forward, startling the woman, who abruptly becomes silent and stops cutting the cake.

'I'm sorry. Are you Hilda?'

'Maybe.'

'The secretary sent me. I'm doing some research here.'

The woman nods. 'I'm Hilda.'

'My name is Kath. The secretary —'

'Ruth.' Hilda snickers.

'She thought I might be able to find a cup of coffee here.'

Hilda pauses, then says, 'Then this is your lucky day, as I just made a pot. Go sit down and I'll bring you some.'

Kath waits at one of the rectangular tables in the cafeteria. The huge room has cinderblock walls painted a milky blue. Light fixtures resembling bowling balls, round and black with soot, dangle from the high ceiling. Thousands of screaming kids, shy kids, friendly kids and fighting kids have eaten lunch in here. Millions of spitballs have coursed through this room. She remembers her own school days and feels unexpectedly sentimental, even though she hated school as a child, it felt like prison. This one looks like a prison. The cafeteria windows, high up on the walls, are covered with metal grating. Sunlight barely gets through the grimy glass.

Hilda shuffles out with a styrofoam cup of coffee, a little metal pitcher of milk and packets of sugar and sweetener. Apparently she has decided Kath is harmless, and sits down with her. It turns out that Hilda has worked in the Bayonne Public Elementary School cafeteria for thirty-four years, including summer school sessions.

'So quiet,' Hilda says, looking around the cafeteria. 'Can't explain it, but I miss them little monsters.'

'Do you have children of your own?' Kath asks.

'Nah. Never married. Just got them.'

'The kids here, you mean?'

Hilda nods. 'Got a picture collage in the back. If you're interested —'

Kath says, 'I'd love to' and follows her into the kitchen. Way in the back, over a small desk, is a poster-size collage of photographs: kids swimming, running, vaulting, kicking and laughing.

'Kids,' Hilda says, 'year after year, they're the same. Kid from fifty-one looks just like a kid from ninety-one. Guess that's why they call it The Family of Man. Everyone's the same. Year after year. Nothing changes.'

'Do you really remember these kids?' Kath asks.

'Yeah. Maybe it's my curse. But I do.'

'Would you recall a name?'

Hilda looks at her suspiciously. 'What're you looking for, exactly?'

'Pictures of my brother, for a video we're making for his surprise fortieth birthday party.'

'Name?'

'Blitsky. Mike Blitsky.'

Hilda shakes her head, a definite negative. Yet her eyes clearly shine behind the round lenses of her glasses. She says, 'There's only one kid people want to know about from here. Bobst.'

'No, Blitsky.'

'You ain't a Blitsky or a Bobst,' Hilda says. 'There were only boys. Anyhow, you're pretty.'

Kath smiles, openly flattered; this is not a compliment she often hears.

Hilda says, 'Who are you? Why are you looking after them? You must be one a them reporter people that's been coming around since Mike got busted.'

Kath surrenders, 'Okay. But I'm not a reporter, I'm doing reserach for a book. We want to find out something about his early years. Can you help?'

Hilda's wrinkly face beams. 'Hell, I'd love to!' She points to a photo tucked into the edge of the collage. Kath looks closely, and lo and behold, there he is: short and plump and round-faced, standing in front of a group of six tall boys. The boys wear little navy blue suits, black shoes, white shirts and navy beenies; all except for little Mike, that is, who wears nothing but baggy white boxer shorts and a sleeveless T-shirt. They're all about ten years old. Mike holds a trophy and sticks out his tongue. The caption reads: '1963 Glee Club Champions. Mi-chael Bobst, front, with trophy.'

'I know him as Mike Blitsky,' Kath says.

Hilda nods. 'Blitsky's the old name, before the trouble happened. Yup. I've been reading about that Mike Blitsky in the papers lately. Nasty business.' She turns pink with excitement. 'Don't know whatever happened to those other two, though. They weren't so bad as that Mike.'

'Which other two?' Kath opens her notebook and jots down the facts.

'There were three,' Hilda says enthusiastically. 'Three Bobst boys, all of 'em looked about like that, but with clothes.' She points to the picture of Mike, fat and resplendent in his underwear. 'Those other two weren't exhibitionists like that Mike. He was the worst. But then he was the oldest, from the first marriage, so he was around for all the real trouble.'

'Trouble?'

'Ooo-wee! I was a lot younger then, of course. My memory's a lot better about those years than about now. Trick of nature. Who knows? But then this is the kind of thing you don't forget. That Mike, his mother set no good example. She ended up in jail for attempted murder. Assaulted her husband. Knocked out all his teeth with a sledgehammer. Don't know her first name — anyway, she's dead now, died right there in jail, never saw the light of day again. Bobst's the second wife's name, Nellie Bobst. Born and bred right here in Bayonne, just like me. Good woman, Nellie. The father took Nellie's name, so did little Mike and she tried to straighten him out. Then Nellie and Martin — that's the father, toothless and all — had themselves two more sons. I'd swear on my mother's grave that all those boys looked alike. But for all the likeness in their faces, only Mike turned out bad. *Bad.*' Hilda goes pink again. 'But he's the only celebrity this school ever had, and I guess it's better than nothing.'

Kath thanks Hilda profusely and goes off to search the public records with her new knowledge. From then on, it's a breeze; facts are there for the looking. Michael Bobst: born 1954; mother, Betty Blitsky, incarcerated; father, Martin Blitsky, later Bobst; stepmother, Nellie Bobst; brother, Mark R., born 1957; brother, Nathan A., born 1959. Mike had dropped out of high school the year of his mother's death, 1969, and left town. Mark fled after finishing school. Martin, their father, sold the Bobst house two months after Nellie died of a stroke, and also left Bayonne. The only one left unaccounted for is Nathan. He, it seems, disappeared without a trace.

Kath meets Dawn at her apartment that evening and lays out the whole story. Dawn becomes so excited that she temporarily forgets all about her awful life and how lonely she is, how all men ultimately jilt her, how she's over thirty and her biological clock is ticking like a bomb; and how all the good men are either married or stymied by intimacy dysfunction, and all the others are gay and half the available men have AIDS anyway. She forgets all that for the moment, and thinks of how good this new information will be for the Blitsky book. Then, as she pops the cork on a bottle of Beaujolais, the name Marco Bobst surges up from recent memory, and she moans, 'Oh my God, Marco! I feel sick.'

'But Dawn, didn't he tell you he grew up in Brooklyn?'

'He's a liar, remember?'

'True.'

Dawn lies back like a wounded soldier.

'It was over anyway, right?' Kath says, hoping to soothe Dawn, who only gets more upset. 'You shouldn't feel discouraged,' Kath tries. 'This is just a coincidence, Marco being Blitsky's half-brother. What does it really matter? You're better off without him. You'll meet other men. Good men. Men who will love you for the wonderful woman you are.'

'Skip it, Kath. The fact is, I slept with the half-brother of a transvestite pimp who's the son of a psycho. How would that make you feel?'

Admittedly, bad. But Kath will not contribute to Dawn's depression, feeling that her duty as a friend is to offer hope and cheer. So she says, 'I would chalk it up to life experience, and move on.'

Dawn smirks, and says, 'Ha!'

Eight
Another Other Woman

Dawn pushes her way through the dark crowded bar. An old-time swing band plays in the next room. Searching through the smoky fog, she locates Andy, sitting alone at a small table, waiting for her.

He says, 'Hi. I'm glad you could make it.'

'Well,' she says, 'here I am.'

Andy smiles and nods. Curly dark hairs sprout from under the V-neck of his red cotton sweater. She suppresses a yearning to suggest that he might have worn an under-shirt. Politely smiling, she sits across from him.

'I hope you're not hungry yet,' he says.

Automatically, she answers, 'Not at all.' A lie. She's starved, and had hoped they would go on to dinner right away.

The waiter comes by — a young man in jeans and a T-shirt that says SAVE THE RAINFOREST — and takes their order: red wine for Dawn, and vodka and tonic for Andy.

'So,' says Andy.

Dawn says, 'So.'

And they both stare off into space: at the band of lean, wrinkled men blowing on their horns; at the crowd of people filling the room; at the waiters as they maneuver with difficulty among the tables and bodies. Now and then, Dawn cops a look at Andy. In the dark, with a little wine traveling through her veins, he doesn't look so bad. According to Hank, Andy is a womanizer, a ruthless businessman, a real operator. Forewarned is forearmed, she thinks; maybe she'll have just a little fling with him. He seems friendly, smart and relatively personable. And in his own way he's even kind of cute: his face is very round, with dimples set in jowls, thinning brown hair and thick black eyebrows, a large rounded nose with a few hairs poking out of the nostrils, and thin, soft lips. Seated, he doesn't look as small as he did the first time she met him. It must be his short legs.

He leans forward on his elbows and peers earnestly at her through squinting eyes. For a minute she thinks there is something wrong with him, then she understands that he's trying to be romantic.

'You look beautiful,' he says. 'Just gorgeous.'

'Thanks,' she says quickly, feeling deeply embarrassed. For a womanizer, she thinks, he isn't very good with women. She sips her wine and watches the band. She can feel him staring at her as if she's the centerfold in the *Sports Illustrated* bathing suit issue, though she doubts her loose madras sundress and flat leather sandals are really that scintillating. She looks at him just long enough to catch a crooked little smile.

'They're engaged, you know,' he says.

She can't resist asking, as if she doesn't know, 'Who?'

'Hank and Chris.'

Hank and Chris. Nausea suddenly tugs at her stomach.

'That's right,' he says. 'She's wearing an engagement ring these days.'

'Oh?'

'Diamonds and emeralds.'

'Teardrop? Set in platinum?'

'That's it.'

That *is* it: Dawn's engagement ring, which she mailed back to Hank in an envelope after he left her. How could he have given it to Chris? Even Dawn would never have expected that of him.

Andy drums his chunky fingers on the wooden table to the rhythm of the music. Dawn forces back a rising, familiar agony. She can't hear about *Hank and Chris* without plunging into depression. Yet here sits Andy, who knows them; it's too much to resist asking him for more information, anything to understand what went wrong that recent night with her beloved Hank.

'How did you meet him?' she asks, trying to sound casual; but despite herself, her voice has that tinny, insecure tone.

'Through Chris.'

'How long have you known her?'

'Let's see. I could tell you I met her through business, but that wouldn't wash because our lines of work don't coincide.'

'Right.'

'I could say that I met her at a dinner party.'

'You could.'

'Nah, it would be a lie too. The truth is, I met little Chrissie years ago in a nightclub. She was wearing an incredibly short black leather miniskirt with black fishnet stockings and these really high heels. It's not that she has the greatest legs, but she looked so dangerous.' He smiles and Dawn notices a slight gap between his front teeth. 'I had to follow her. From the back it looked like she wasn't wearing a shirt. When she turned around I saw it was this little thing, like a bathing suit top or a bra, but less. She was sensational. We talked. We danced. She came home with me — her suggestion. We were lovers for a week or two. Then, who knows? She disappeared,' he snaps his fingers, 'like that.'

Every word is like a hammer, pounding in the awful truth. Chris is a seductress, a temptress, she is exactly what Dawn is not. Dawn is just an average good person, the kind you can find anywhere; she must have bored Hank to death. Maybe she should spice up her wardrobe a little, she thinks, and decides to seriously consider it. And just at that moment — at the part about Chris's fishnet stockings, which is about the time Dawn veers off into ruminations about her own style of dressing — she catches a glimpse of someone across the room. He's handsome. He's got great blue eyes. He's Jack! But where is Kath? And who is that woman seated across from him?

Andy just barely finishes his monologue when Dawn leaves him and strides across the room. By the time she reaches Jack's table, he has spotted her, and watches her approach with obvious trepidation.

His companion turns around and looks at Dawn. The girl is very young, twenty maybe, with long brown hair and a perky face under a lot of makeup. She's got on a flouncy red silk blouse and dangling beaded earrings.

'Hijack,' Dawn says.

His face pales. 'Hi,' he says. 'How are you?'

'Fine,' she says. 'So, how's Kath?' And with that, she looks directly at the girl.

'This is Joanna,' Jack says. 'She's an English major at Barnard.'

'What a coincidence. Kath studies English, too.'

'Oh really?' says Joanna. 'What year is she in? I wonder if we've had any classes together.'

'I'm sure you haven't. Kath is in the doctorate program. She's much older than you, about Jack's and my age. Thirty something or other.'

'But Jack's only twenty-five,' she says, looking at Jack as if to confirm this blatant misinformation.

'Twenty-five? Wait til Kath hears this. You're such a joker, Jack!'

Jack looks like he wants to murder Dawn. And she looks back at him with a similar passion.

'Joanna and I just met to —' he starts to say.

'We met ten days ago. It happened so fast.' She smiles at him. 'Wanna join us?'

'Oh, no thanks, I've got a ... you know . . . over there.'

She lifts her chin to indicate the other half of the room. Andy watches them with great interest.

'Well, Jack. I guess I'll be seeing you.'

Jack nods and smiles a taut, sad smile. A miserable smile of defeat, loss, heartache and regret. A beautiful smile.

Jack says, 'It was nice to see you, Dawn. Maybe we could talk later? Or tomorrow?'

'Sure,' she answers. He has her hooked with his gorgeous blue eyes: the color of sky, of ocean, of sapphires. His eyes have shot a little needle of sympathy into her heart for his peculiar male plight, though she cannot begin to understand it.

She returns to the table, no longer a casual, attractive woman on a Saturday night date, but a New Age adult in the throes of a moral dilemma.

What to do?

Her impulse is to go straight for the phone, call Kath and deliver the newsflash: your boyfriend is cheating on you. But how can she? Kath would be devastated. Could there be some way to spare her the awful pain of infidelity? Dawn takes a deep breath and closes her eyes. She can feel Andy staring, clearly wondering what the hell is wrong with her. Her mind reels. What about Jack? She barely knows him, but he had seemed like such a nice guy. Yet here he is, right before her eyes, on a date with someone else. Isn't she obliged to tell Kath about this? Or maybe she should try to reason with Jack?

'Hey, babe, what's the scoop?' Andy says, and Dawn feels like punching him out. 'Interested in a little Cajun food?'

'Actually — I'm having a really great time, Andy — but I think I have a headache and I'd like to go on home, if you don't mind.'

'I'm game.'

That's not what she meant. She wants to go home alone.

'The truth is, Andy, well this is hard to say, but I think I'd like to be alone tonight. You see, something upsetting just happened, and I need to think.'

Andy turns like a whip to Jack and sizes him up, then looks back to Dawn. 'Yes, I see,' he says. She is aware that he most probably misunderstands the situation but doesn't care. She has one objective: to get home without passing Cajun restaurant, without passing big seduction scene, without passing out from drinking on an empty stomach. Home, to think, to decide the fate of Kath's heart.

Andy says, 'I'll take you home, then.' He pays the bill and follows her outside, where the cool breeze is a surprising relief after all that smoke.

'Let's walk,' Dawn says, 'if you don't mind.'

'Not at all.'

They walk down Broadway. The mood is predominantly that of an evening promenade: people strolling arm-in-arm, eating ice-cream cones, New Yorkers not-going-anywhere, just walking off a good weekend meal. Dawn and Andy walk at a brisker pace, in silence.

As angst blossoms exponentially in her troubled mind, Dawn finds herself wondering why Andy isn't making any attempt to hold her hand or weave an arm around her waist, as you would expect from a womanizer. Isn't she attractive, desirable, special? she wonders. After years of experience, with some psychotherapy thrown in, she ought to know by now that self-doubt is a cry of insecurity, not to be heeded as a call to action. But in her muddled and somewhat intoxicated state, it does not occur to her that perhaps his strategy is to incite insecurity so as to make her want his advances for reassurance. Dawn, lost in the Kath/Jack moral dilemma, doesn't get Andy's angle.

They reach Dawn's building, and Andy says, 'Too bad we couldn't do dinner. Maybe another time.'

'Maybe another time,' she echoes in a wavering tone that belies her lack of confidence. Then, impulsively, she offers, 'I guess if you want you could come up and we could order Chinese food.'

'Maybe,' he says. 'But I can't stay long, I have to be up early tomorrow.'

They select dinner from a take-out menu, and Dawn speed-dials in their order. She pours them some wine and they wait for the food. As Andy tells her about his workplace, she thinks about Kath and Jack and Joanna, until the doorbell snaps her back to the present. She rushes to the door with her purse (Andy conveniently visits the bathroom at this time) and dishes the food onto plates in the kitchen. They sit side by side on the couch, plates balanced on knees.

Andy is adept at eating cold sesame noodles with chopsticks. Strangely, she begins to find him attractive, something about the way he twirls the gummy noodles into a neat clump and pops the whole thing into his mouth with a few efficient chews and a big, satisfied swallow. The attraction is tucked away in the back of her mind, though. She isn't consciously thinking about sex, only subconsciously, which puts her in dangerous territory, as the subconscious doesn't know from sexually transmitted diseases and therefore does not plan ahead and buy condoms.

Andy finishes a heaping plate of lemon chicken and Buddhas Delight, then lies back into the couch. 'So,' he says, 'do you want to tell me what's wrong?'

Dawn looks at him: small and soft and open. If he turns out to be a nice, sensitive guy, it will ruin everything. The point is not to fall in love with someone new, or have a one-night-stand, or anything like that. The point is to get back to basics: to help Kath, and either forget about Hank or get him back into her life, whichever comes first.

'Come here, I'll rub your temples,' he says. Without thinking about it, deciding either yes or no, she zeros in on the offered sensation. She stands up, goes around the coffee table and sits next to him. He rubs her temples in slow, firm circles that feel really good. And then — swoosh — his hands are on her breasts and she lets him. And she touches him, too. They start to move together rhythmically and twine their bodies, and she tells herself, oh well, here goes, it's too late to stop now.

But Andy's body won't start; like an old engine in the freezing cold, it just grinds a little and then dies down. Dawn is mildly relieved. She sits up next to him, yawns and says, 'That's okay, I'm kind of tired. Feel like seeing what's on TV?'

Andy sighs. 'Maybe I should just go?'

Dawn looks at him sitting there, slumped into the couch, ashamed. She would prefer to be left alone, but now she feels sorry for him. So she says, 'No, stay. There's probably a good old movie on the tube, we can snuggle up and watch it.'

They repair to the bedroom like an old, tired couple whose sex life is far in the past. Luckily, they find a fifties Doris Day/ Rock Hudson farce about a married couple in the suburbs, and watch that. Eventually, they fall asleep.

Nine
A Silver Smile

Jack's curly blond hair glistens wet from the shower, drying quickly in the hot morning air. He wears jeans, battered sneakers and a red T-shirt with a motley green earth silk-screened on the front, looking like a freelancer or comfortably unemployed, as he walks three blocks from the subway to the shabby brick warehouse of Katz's Scene Shop. He uses his key to open the graffitied metal door. Opera blares. Mel's already here. Early — it figures — even on Sunday morning.

The new show has been nothing but trouble. Mel called Jack late last night to ask him to come in today. Jack likes his job, and Mel's really not that bad, so he agreed. 'Sure, Mel, I'll be there at —' he was going to say 'about noon' when Mel said, 'Ten o'clock, sharp.' So, here Jack is, on his way to the scene shop instead of getting the *Times* and warm bagels as usual. It's a good thing he didn't bring Joanna home with him last night; she wouldn't have been too happy about this. But then, if he had gone with her to her apartment as she had wanted, Mel wouldn't have reached him last night, and Dawn wouldn't have reached him this morning. Anyway, he really wasn't in the mood to sleep with Joanna, not after that episode in the bar. She's a nice girl, but not worth losing Kath over. But how can he jump into life with Kath, both feet first? He'll lose control. He has got to keep one foot planted firmly in his own life, his private life, maintain his independence, keep himself balanced. He is only thirty-one. Is a man of such youth actually expected to make a commitment to one woman? Maybe even get married and have babies?

No!

The cavernous warehouse echoes with 'La Traviata'. A sour smell of paint hits Jack; evidently, a couple of the other guys got in even earlier. He walks past a backdrop of hilly, green Ireland superimposed with a graph of low stone walls that haven't been painted in yet. Next to that, three city stoops, then a medieval castle with a half-open drawbridge, then a luxurious living room with a birdseye view of the Eiffel Tower.

'Who's there?' Mel's voice echoes, followed by footsteps punctuating the pulse and sweep of doleful operatic song. A loud creaking sound and *voila*, Mel.

Mel Katz is a small, boxy man in denim overalls. Light shines off the bald spot in the middle of his head, which is surrounded by a halo of white hair. He has tiny eyes and a small, flat nose. When he sees Jack, he smiles that weird silver smile of his: two neat, even rows of glistening tombstones.

'You're late, Green,' Mel says.

If Jack didn't know better, he'd panic, but he's been with Mel for three years now and knows the man is peculiar. He looks at his watch, a blue Swatch with a jagged yellow lightning bolt racing down its face. It is 10:02.

'Sorry, Mel,' Jack says. 'Just couldn't drag myself out of bed.'

'Yeah, yeah, yeah,' says Mel. 'Danny pissed in his pants when he saw the witness box you built Friday.'

'What exactly is bothering him?'

'Check it out, Green. Lean on it once and I bet you it'll split apart. Make it sturdy. Deadline's next week.'

'Okay,' Jack says. 'You're the boss.'

'You betcha.'

'Well, I better get started. I've got a lunch date at one, Mel, just so you know. I'm gonna have to take a break.'

Jack puts on his paint-splattered denim overalls and Mel stands there, watching. It's easy to tell when Mel's formulating a thought, which often comes out as a bad joke. He has the lousiest sense of humor.

'So,' says Mel. 'I'm standing here, and Danny says to his boy assistant, he says, "Yo, Paul, why ain't condoms black?"'

Danny, Jack knows, does not talk like that at all. He's highly refined and well educated. He speaks correctly. Plus, he has the gay accent.

'And Paul, he says, "I dunno. Why not?" And Danny, he says, "Because black thins." Ha ha ha ha ha!'

Jack stares at Mel, whose laughter echoes like the twinging of a distant ping pong ball.

'Ya didn't get it, did ya?' Mel says.

Jack says, 'No.'

'Black *thins*.'

Oh. Women wear black dresses because it makes them look thinner. And who wants his erection to look thinner? That's why condoms aren't black. Ha. . . .

'I guess I'll get started,' Jack says.

'Yeah,' Mel mumbles. 'And this time, do it right. Mistakes cost money.'

Jack goes to the other end of the huge warehouse, to reinforce the witness box in the courtroom set for a new play that will probably close on opening night, anyway. But Jack likes what he's doing. It's fun, like playing, not working. Before he worked for Mel, he waited tables, drove a cab, was an apprentice electrician, and for six months drove a truck for a road production of'A Chorus Line.' He heard about Katz's Scene Shop from one of the other roadies. Working here at the scene shop these last few years, life has been a little more stable. Anyway, he is keenly aware that, as he's only thirty-one, he has plenty of time to decide what to do with his life.

Jack works. The time passes quickly and one o'clock comes and goes. Meanwhile, Dawn knocks on the front door and no one hears her over the blaring opera. Finally, she lets herself in and shouts: 'Hello? Hello? Anyone here? I'm looking for Jack Green. Jack? Hello?'

Mel appears. He says, 'Whaddya want?' She smiles. He doesn't. He enjoys frightening new people. 'Yeah?'

'I'm looking for a friend.'

'You mean to tell me you got friends?'

'Who are you?'

He taps his foot on the floor, creating a series of quick echoes. 'Mel Katz,' he says. 'Who are you?'

'Dawn Waterston,' she says in her professional tone of voice. 'May I please see Jack Green?'

He stands there like a rock and stares at her. Finally, he says, 'Jack's woikin'.'

'Look, Mr. Katz—'

He cracks a silver smile. 'I'm lookin'.'

Agitated and a little frightened now, she turns and walks toward the door with steps that echo like sharp slaps.

Katz calls out, 'Green, you gotta visitor!'

Dawn stops. She stands right where she is, and waits.

Jack jogs over. 'Hey, Dawn!' He can see that she's upset and checks his watch: it's one-fifteen. Maybe she's been talking to Mel for a little while. She shoots a look at Mel, and Jack knows he's right.

'Keep it short, Green,' Mel says.

Jack rolls his eyes. Dawn stands like a statue, frozen, as if she can't decide whether to stay and talk to Jack, or just leave. She is wearing a white T-shirt, a white cotton skirt with vertical blue stripes, and red polish on her toes at which Mel stares with no shame.

'Okay, Mel. Half an hour.'

'Yeah, yeah, yeah,' Mel grumbles, and finally goes away.

'Is he always like that?' Dawn asks.

'Unfortunately.'

'Well, I guess we don't have much time. Can we sit?'

Jack leads her to the stoop of an urban backdrop. She stares at it. 'But it isn't real,' she says. 'It's painted on.'

'Just kidding. Follow me.'

They cross to the far corner of the warehouse, to the courtroom set. Dawn gets the one chair, and Jack pulls up a paint can on which he squats, a big man sitting on a teeny little can. Such is life.

'All right,' Dawn says. 'What's going on?'

'I don't know.'

She sighs. 'I didn't come all the way out to Brooklyn to hear "I don't know." I saw you with someone else. Kath lov . . . she really cares about you, Jack. She takes you *seriously*.'

Maybe she stopped herself from saying the L word, thinking that Kath hasn't said it to him herself. But she has. They have said the L word to each other. Jack knows in his heart that Kath loves him, and she seems to know that he really loves her. But if Dawn spills the beans about Joanna, Kath won't trust him. He is aware of the seriousness of that.

He shrugs. 'I don't love Joanna,' he says. 'It was just a ... I don't know.'

Dawn gives him one of those looks, incredulity narrowing her eyes, impatience puckering her mouth, frustration erupting into a sigh. 'Kath is my best friend. It's bound to come out sooner or later that you're not being exclusive. And it's also bound to come out, one way or another, that I knew about it. We'd both lose her. I don't want that, do you?'

'No.'

'Then —'

'I just can't make a commitment to her right now!' Jack blurts so loudly it echoes. Lowering his voice, he says, 'When I think about it, I feel like I can't breathe. I cannot do it. I have to feel free.'

'What about Kath?'

'I'm crazy about Kath.'

'Does she know that?'

'Yes.'

'Has she told you how she feels about you?'

His eyes flicker before settling on Dawn's earnest face. A sweet coil of feeling tightens in him. Kath, her soft pale body stretched next to him, her long black hair loose, entangling them. Her whispers of love, of happiness, of relief. He says, 'Yes.'

'I don't have to tell Kath about this.'

Jack's heart jumps. 'Really? You won't?'

'But you do.'

'Right.'

'Are you going to see that girl again?'

Jack shrugs.

Dawn sighs.

'Look, Jack, it's none of my business what you do, but I won't lie to Kath. If you're going to deal with this — say good-bye to *her* and talk to Kath — then I swear, I won't say a word about it. But if you go on seeing that girl, and I know about it, how can I just let Kath stay in her little fantasy about this great relationship she's having?'

'Is that what she thinks?'

'Of course that's what she thinks!'

'Okay, okay, okay. I guess she has every reason to.'

'You're damn right she does.'

'I fucked up.'

'You sure did. So?'

'I will. I'll give up Joanna. I'll talk to Kath.'

Dawn looks surprised. 'You will?'

Jack nods. 'Absolutely. I have to if I want to keep Kath, right?'

'Yes, I think you do.'

'Then I'll take care of it.'

'Good.'

'Tonight.'

'Jack, you're doing the right thing.'

Ha! He knows he is going to do what is right for him, to have what he wants, when he wants it. He is a man, and a man must do what a man must do — at least he is wont to do what he wants to do.

'Thanks for talking, Dawn. And really, thanks for not saying anything to Kath. I'll handle it.'

Dawn looks as relieved as Jack suddenly feels frantic. He could go ahead and do what he just told Dawn he's going to do, simplify things, be straight about it. Or he could not do that. The alternatives truly frighten him.

'I guess I'll be getting back to the city,' Dawn says, standing. 'You know, Jack, I like you. I hope you two can work it out.'

Jack smiles, and also stands. 'Thanks!' he says in the overly confident tone of a scared man and soon-to-be-proven liar.

As he walks her to the door, the loud music fades and a voice — Katz, who else? — says: 'The sun rose and it was Dawn.'

A spatter of applause, probably his own, fills the warehouse. Someone laughs. Dawn laughs, too.

'Weird guy,' she says.

'That's for sure.'

'Bye, Jack. See you around, I hope.' She stands in the open door with bright June sunlight sizzling behind her.

'Bye,' he says. 'And don't worry.'

Ten
A Man Among Men

Kath snips the air with a big pair of sewing scissors. 'Jack *loves* my hair.'

'Don't do it.'

'But Dawn . . . .' Kath cries as she cuts. Sheets of her long black hair fall into the sink and on the floor. 'I should have known something like this would happen. It was too good.' She grabs a last handful of hair, and with one clean bite of the scissors, twelve inches tumble down.

Dawn's face looms behind Kath in the medicine chest mirror. She looks pale and disturbed, while Kath's face is bright red and salty wet, her eyes swollen.

'How could he do this to me?' she sobs.

I know how you feel, but Jack didn't break up with you, not exactly.'

'He told me he wants to see other women. How can I keep seeing him now? I love him. How can I share him?'

'Kath — look at you!'

And she does, and she's shocked at how awful she looks. She cries even harder. With her chopped, uneven hair, she looks like a Barbie doll that's been ravished by a mad scissor-slinging six-year-old. She looks like Laurie Anderson.

'Good job,' Dawn says. 'Are you finished yet?'

Kath cuts a chunk out of her bangs.

Dawn turns off the bathroom light, putting an end to her friend's madness. She goes to the living room and Kath follows, plopping down next to Dr. Johnson, who is stretched long on the couch, airing his white belly. He curls against her side and purrs. Dawn sits at Kath's table, where research papers and books are stacked. It's a hot night. Kath's fan whirrs, ruffling the papers.

'You know, Jack could be back. I wouldn't be surprised. He just needs some extra rope.'

Kath snorts cynical laughter. 'Right. Give them all the rope they want and let them hang themselves. That's what they say.'

'Kath, why don't you see him on his terms for a while? See how it works.'

'It won't work.'

'You don't know that. I wish Hank had given me that option. He left me cold, period, kaput.'

'I hate men!'

'No you don't.'

'Yes I do.'

'You just think they hate you.'

'Don't they?'

'I don't think so. Maybe they hate me, though.'

'Oh, Dawn, you're terrific. You know Hank doesn't hate you, he's just confused. And that Blitsky thing. Hank's such a dyed-in-the-wool careerist. But I bet he'll be back.'

'He's marrying Chris.'

Kath bolts forward and stares at her friend. Her hair stands up on her head in electric clumps. Suddenly, she bursts into tears. 'I just can't believe it!' Dawn sits next to her on the couch and touches her hair. Sobs melt into deep, convulsive breathing. 'Oh God,' she moans, 'now I'll never be able to work on my dissertation. How can I possibly concentrate?'

'Will you take a suggestion?'

'I don't know. Maybe. Depends.'

'See Jack on his terms. Go out with other men, too. It'll drive him crazy. You'll see.'

'It didn't exactly work for you when you tried that.'

'You're a different person. I still think it's a good concept.'

'But I'm in love with Jack.'

'Love is complicated.'

Kath lets out a small, airy laugh. 'I'll think about it,' she says. 'But I couldn't see myself sleeping with someone else. I just don't feel it, I don't want to.'

'Good. I have the perfect person in mind for you. He's nice, and he isn't very sexual. Maybe he could help.'

'Help . . . ' Kath sighs. 'I don't know.'

Dawn leans forward and smiles. 'What are you doing to-morrow night?'

'I feel so uncomfortable,' Kath whispers across the table. 'This dress isn't right for me. It's too tight under the arms. I should have stayed home and gotten some work done. The last two days have been awful. I'm exhausted.'

'Relax,' Dawn says. 'Just try to have a good time.'

But it's hard to have a good time when your heart is broken.

LunaLuna, this week's trendy new spot, is a small room crowded with speckled marble-topped tables and decorated with bunches of rope-tied wheat suspended on the walls. All the waiters and waitresses appear to be under twenty-three, all are dressed in black, all have hairdos much like Kath's —jet-black punky affairs, cropped close to the scalp — and two have numerous earrings climbing their lobes. LunaLuna lunacy, is what Kath thinks. She'd rather be eating falafel in a dive with her beloved Jack. And she feels ridiculous in this outfit, borrowed under duress from Dawn: sleeveless and red with a heavily pleated short skirt, black stockings, and black patent leather high heels that pinch her toes together merci-lessly. Earlier that evening, Dawn took some gel to Kath's hair and combed it to stand straight up, then insisted she wear lipstick called 'Passion Bud'. What if one of the other doctoral students see her? Or, worse yet, Professor Banks, her advisor and mentor?

'I wish I hadn't dressed up for this man,' Kath says. 'I don't even know him.'

'Of course you don't, it's a blind date.'

'Then why are you here, too?'

'To make sure you go through with it.'

And before Kath has a chance to figure out how not to go through with it, her date approaches through a maze of little square tables and diffident waiters. He carries himself with an air of importance, like a man fresh off a private jet. Expensive suit. Polished shoes. Starched shirt. Boldly patterned silk tie. Trench coat over one arm. Briefcase clutched in the other hand.

'Jesus,' Dawn mutters.

And Kath says, 'Oh, no.'

He greets Dawn and then turns his most charming, gap-toothed smile on Kath. So this is the man who is supposed to help her care less about Jack.

'Meet Andy Shoemaker,' Dawn says.

'Ladies,' Andy says with a nod of his head. He is clearly a man who enjoys having more than one woman on his arm, as if it demonstrates virility, or desirability, or date-ability, or at the very least the capacity of his wallet. He pulls out a chair and sits. He beams at Kath.

Images of Jack's face, when he finds out about her dating other men, flash into her mind: Jack begging her not to; Jack promising not to, either, if she stops; Jack remorseful, repentant. True love, marriage, babies, a Sunday morning lazy bed full of newsprint, coffee smells and familiar bodies. Andy has a nice smile, Kath thinks, which is something she could definitely use at the moment.

Kath is cool and that makes Andy nervous, which puts Kath right in the driver's seat. It's good to be the one in control. She knows that in the game of love — when it is more game than love — the ball bounces in one person's court at a time. Sometimes it dribbles there indefinitely. She watches it bounce around her feet, while he waits impatiently for her to toss it over. She suspects that for him, the challenge is the lure. He takes her out, buys her flowers, walks her home, and when he asks to sleep with her, she flatly refuses. They are dating, she reminds him, the old-fashioned way; which, she insists, is the New Age AIDS-crazed thing to do.

Meanwhile, Jack pops in and out of her life, and Kath feels oddly vindicated in being able to casually decline him now and then, saying: ' Can't, have a date tonight.' This drives him mad but he won't admit it. The closest he comes to any overt reaction to the change in their relationship is when he sees her new hairdo.

Visibly stunned, he asks, 'What happened?'

She shoots him a bitter look. 'I felt like cutting it.'

He rushes to her and runs his hands through her hair, a desperate man. 'Jeez, look at it,' he says. 'But it's so soft.'

Kath coolly allows him to fondle her head, deliberately not responding to the intense attraction she feels for him. His kelly green T-shirt delineates his sculpted chest, which she yearns to touch, but does not. She grips her knees with fingers aching to feel the stubble on his face. As he gently rubs his palm along her choppy hair, she feels overcome by a wave of love. She feels sure he must love her; no man can look at a woman with intent, blazing eyes like that and not love her.

If only he didn't love whats-her-name too.

She reminds herself to keep busy, move on, make the man think he's going to lose her if he doesn't start shaping up. She reminds herself that love is work, and once you've got it, the rest is maintenance.

His fingers travel from her hair to her face, where they tenderly explore. Tears well up in Kath's eyes and fall down her cheeks. Jack wipes them away with strong and gentle thumbs. He kisses her cheek, her temple, her ear, her eye, her nose, her mouth.

'I love you,' he whispers.

'Don't,' she says, and pushes him away.

She's got a date that night, and because Jack doesn't argue when she tells him it's time to leave, she assumes he has plans, too.

Andy. She has never used someone before and finds that it is surprisingly easy. All you have to do is go out with them and pretend to like them a little more than you really do, and somehow manage to fool your own better judgment. So far, on all their dates, they have gone to restaurants and movies and taken walks and had conversations. Dating. And that is how it goes, until....

Andy makes a request. He says, 'I bet you didn't know I could cook. I want to show off my cooking to you. I've heard the way to a woman's heart is through her stomach.'

Kath realizes that meeting him on his own territory is inevitable, and that she has probably put it off as long as possible. Though she feels wildly nervous about it, she accepts.

On the afternoon of Andy's dinner, Jack homes in on her like radar detecting trouble. She is sitting at her table, surrounded by books, reading and taking notes. Dr. Johnson responds to the intercom buzzer before she does, walking to his post at the door. Kath jolts out of concentration. She is expecting no one. When she asks into the intercom, 'Who's there?' and hears back, 'Me, Jack,' she feels momentarily shocked, then happy. She cracks open the door, and Dr. Johnson positions himself. She returns to her seat at the table and listens to his thumping footsteps coming up the stairs. Enter Jack, holding a yellow rose, a six-pack of beer, and wearing a big smile. Kath bounds out of her seat and rushes to him, hugs him, kisses him. She feels like Cinderella being saved at the eleventh hour by the right prince. Is Dawn's idea working?

'Hi,' he says, holding her tightly. 'I'm glad you're home.'

'Me too.'

Kath takes the rose and goes to the kitchen for a glass of water to put it in. He follows her with the beer, which he puts in the refrigerator. She feels a small thrill at the way he does this, with familiarity; it pleases her that he knows where things are in her kitchen. She turns to him and smiles, drawing him to her. He kisses her gently, and she can't move for the pleasure. In her mind, the geometry of this day has instantly altered, and she now assumes she will spend it, into the night, with Jack.

They open two beers and return to the living room, where the fan makes a cool swishing breeze. Sitting on the couch, holding her hand, he asks, 'So, how's your week been?'

She shrugs. 'Okay. Uneventful.' Lies. She's had an awful, lonely week, even though Andy took her to the opening of a Broadway play. 'How about you?'

'Same,' he says. 'I've missed you.'

'I've missed you, too.'

And presto, they're in bed. Fully condomized, they rock and tumble and kiss and carress and stop and start and spend the afternoon. Then, they sit naked on the bed and drink the rest of the beer.

Kath is lost to this love, to the rush of feeling Jack brings her, to their sex. She stretches luxuriously, her limbs tangling with his. They roll together into a hug.

'Feel like seeing a movie tonight?' she says.

Jack tenses; she can feel his whole body go cold and distant. 'Actually,' he says, rolling over and sitting up, 'I have some plans.'

Kath says, coolly, 'Actually, so do I.'

Andy answers the door in his little red bathrobe. She ignores this obviously deliberate indiscretion, and walks in, saying, 'Well, I'm here.'

'Excellent! Hungry?'

Kath says, 'Starved.' She smiles, viscerally recalling the sweet afternoon, and the bitterness of Jack's leaving.

'Sorry I'm not dressed,' he says, 'but I just finished rowing.'

'Rowing?'

'On my rowing machine,' he says. 'I'll show you.'

She follows him down a long narrow hallway, behind his swaying red-clad hips. His squat, hairy legs are fully exposed beneath his minirobe. They come to the living room: faded white walls hung with framed prints; bookshelves crammed with classics; photos of family and friends tacked to the wall. Pushed up next to the brown corduroy couch is a strange contraption of chrome bars and Naugahyde pads.

'There,' Andy points to the thing. 'My rowing machine. It keeps me fit.'

As long as he feels good about himself, she thinks, that's all that counts.

'Something smells good,' Kath says, changing the subject lest he disrobe so she can examine his physique for the results of his rowing.

'*Poutlet a la creme de Dijon,*' he says. 'I was about to shower. Would you mind stirring the sauce?'

Kath says, 'Lead the way,' glad at the prospect of being left alone, yet aware that, as most people shower before a date, Andy must be maneuvering.

He takes her back down the hall and into the kitchen. On the way, they pass his bedroom — he has left the door wide open to reveal a bed made up with dove grey sheets and covered with a red blanket — and the bathroom. The kitchen is small and cluttered, with a table and four chairs taking up much of the space. The counters are crowded with a Cuisinart, a microwave, an espresso machine, a blender, a toaster and other domestic appliances. By the look of things, Andy really does like to cook. She begins to wonder if perhaps this is really nothing but a dinner invitation, after all.

He says, 'Back in a flash,' and leaves the kitchen.

She goes to the stove and peeks into the steaming pots and pans until she locates some coagulated yellowish stuff that is the closest thing to sauce. She finds a spoon and stirs. A lot of time seems to pass. Finally, she abandons the sauce and goes looking for him.

The bathroom door is wide open and the shower is running. And there is Andy, dry as a bone, standing next to the tub, stark naked. Her heart jumps: Andy Shoemaker, disrobed. Surprisingly, he isn't badly built. He stares at her, daring her; he wants her to check him out, so she does. Most people look fatter out of clothes than in them, but Andy looks firmer and trimmer in the nude. By the way his chest is puffed out, he appears to be holding in his stomach, which is large but flat. For a short man, he looks strikingly long. His legs are thin and finely muscled. His arms are roundish. His whole body, from neck to ankle, is covered with dark, downy hair.

'I think the sauce is ready,' she says.

He parts the shower curtain and steps in. Then he pokes his head out and says, 'Care to join me?'

Without answering, she rushes to the living room.

Let the sauce burn!

She makes herself a gin and tonic. With all the alcohol already in her system, the drink doesn't take long to sock into effect. She relaxes into the couch, puts her feet up on the coffee table, rests her head back and dreams a better dream than the reality of what this day has become.

When Andy appears — dressed, finally — she lifts her glass and says, 'I helped myself.' He sits down next to her and plants a kiss smack on her lips. Through the haze of gin, the kiss actually feels good. It feels, in fact, like Jack. Her mind jolts from thought to thought, sensation to sensation, memory to memory, as Andy's tongue explores the inside of her mouth. All of a sudden she becomes very hot. Then her mind goes completely numb.

Kath's initial instinct was right: she never should have come. And did she bring condoms? *No.*

He stands and tries to tug her up.

This has never happened to her before, two men in one day. She has never even had two men in one year. Although the Age of Adventure is over, Kath can't help regretting just a little that she missed it; and she decides, in a post-sexual-revolution drunken flash, to go with the experience.

'Andy,' she mutters, 'do you have any protection?'

He smiles. 'In the bedroom.'

They go to the bedroom, to the bed. He kisses her, while clumsily searching for the hook at the back of her bra.

'Here,' she says, expertly snapping her bra apart in the front.

Andy appears shocked. He stares at the bra like it's some kind of strange animal. Kath demonstrates how it works, and as he tries unsnapping it himself, she laughs.

'What's so funny?' He shifts away and looks at her suspiciously.

'The bra,' Kath says. 'I just thought it was cute that you didn't know how to work it. Why?'

'Oh nothing, nothing,' he says. He rolls over and pulls the sheet up over his belly.

She runs her hand under the sheet and feels; stomach, groin, penis. Limp.

'We don't have to,' she says.

And he replies, 'Yes, we do.'

Andy, in the end, is not a bad lover, though he's not a particularly good lover either. At least not for Kath. She can barely believe she's in bed with him after the incredible afternoon with Jack. An awareness that she is betraying herself swims through the blotted haze of her brain; but at the moment, she cannot begin to feel the impact of it.

In the morning, she wakes up alone in bed. The red bathrobe is on the floor. She picks it up, shakes it out and puts it on. Her head is throbbing. She needs coffee, fast.

She follows the sound of heavy breathing to the living room, and there he is, sitting on the rowing machine, pulling the handles back and forth and sweating up a storm.

'Morning,' he chokes.

It strikes Kath as strange that Andy should be up early, rowing away, with a new lover languishing in his bed. Expecially after all the eagerness and effort that went into con-summating his long wait. They never even got to dinner last night. Then it strikes her as even stranger to think of herself as Andy's lover. She stands there and watches him row, his tubby stomach rippling. In her post-alcohol, pre-coffee, morning daze, she can't tell what she feels for this man. Except maybe nothing.

'There's coffee in the kitchen,' he gasps.

Pouring coffee into one of Andy's brown mugs, Kath is stung with a sudden thought of Jack. Where is he this morning? She sips her coffee and quickly revives. Jack put her up to all this. She's doing it for Jack.

She'll get him back even if she has to sleep with Andy again.

The minute Kath gets home, she dials Jack. 'Hello?' 'Hi.'

'I tried calling you before. . . .'

'I was out.'

'Library?'

'I had a date last night.'

'A date?'

'Yeah, you know, this guy I met.'

'Oh.'

'I had a good time.' Liar!

'Good.'

'What did you do?'

'I, uh, had a date too.'

She feels the twist of jealousy, and says, calmly, 'Well, that was the arrangement.'

'It was,' he says. And she can hear the same twist in his voice. And she knows: it's working.

Eleven
A Woman at Heart

Dawn hangs up the phone. Now this really pisses her off! How is it that Andy had an erection with Kath, and not with her? Life is not fair, and the more it goes on, the less fair it is to Dawn. She gazes around her office, which at her worst moments feels like a cell, incarceration without trial. She didn't give up life for her career; life gave her up, and her career is all she has left. She loves her work, but also wants to get married and have kids. Since when is that too much to ask?

Tony comes into her office and drops the Blitsky manuscript on her desk. 'Proofed.'

'Now I have to get Blitsky's final approval on the new changes,' Dawn says. 'I'm a little worried he won't sign off on it now. Did you get through to him?'

'Left a message on his machine.' Tony rolls his eyes. *'At Misled Mike's, the customer always comes first.'*

'Yuck!'

'I mean, I'm gay, and I'm no prude, but even I think he's perverted.'

'Well, you're more conservative than most of the straight people I know.'

'Do you really think so?' Tony seems flattered.

Dawn smiles. She wishes she could keep him forever, like a pet; but he's proven himself as her assistant and she knows he'll have to be promoted after a year, maybe two.

'So, any word on pushing back the pub date?' she asks.

'Janice says she'll work on it. Anyway, the art department could use more time, but they'll need to know if you want to rush it through for Christmas.'

'Fucking Christmas.'

'Now now, Dawn.'

'I'm going to be alone this Christmas.' Dawn feels like crying at the thought. It's going to be awful. Her whole family will be scrutinizing her, thinking "That Dawn just can't hold her man." 'Maybe I won't go.'

'Maybe you'll find someone new, and then you can spend the holidays with him. Think positive.' He winks.

'Right.' Dawn fans the edge of the five-hundred thirty-six-page manuscript.

'What now?'

Dawn sighs. 'I have to call Hank,' she says. 'I dread it. I don't know why I ever agreed to postpone the book. Pre-trial sales would be a boon.'

'Love.'

'What?'

'You did it because you love him.'

'Hank Lowe? He's got a penis for a brain! All I care about is getting this goddamn book to publication and taking my vacation.'

'Yes, dear. Do you need anything else now?'

'No,' she says. 'Sorry, Tony.'

He shuts her door so she can sulk in private before placing the dreaded call. She reminds herself to act like a professional, no matter what Hank does, says, implies, suggests, or doesn't do, say, imply, or suggest. She must keep her cool. She must not think of her ring on Chris's skinny, red-clawed finger. She must visualize positive things, like . . . like . . . well, like a bowl of chocolate chip ice cream and the return of *thirtysomething*.

She takes three deep breaths, and dials.

* * *

Carla's voice rasps through the intercom: 'It's Dawn.'

Hank hates it when she calls him; he prefers to place the call himself, so as to be cool, calm and collected when they speak. He's always depressed after speaking with her, and when she catches him off guard, it can be devastating. Guilt. Shame. What can he possibly say about Chris? How can he explain his reasons for having given her the ring? He doesn't even know what the hell he's doing; all he knows is that he's following Chris's orders and hoping for the best.

'Well?' Carla's voice demands. 'Are you taking the call?'

'Tell her I'm in a meeting. I'll call her back.'

He watches the fire-red light until it blinks off. Then he swivels around in his chair and gazes down upon the hot July crowd on Park Avenue. The human throng; how simple it all looks from way up here .... *Calm yourself*, he mentally intones, *and attend to business.* He reminds himself that he is a legal warrior, that he will do what he must do. *Call Dawn* —just give it half an hour or so to substantiate the lie about being in a meeting.

He reroutes his anxiety toward an inspection of reality. The Blitsky case is going as planned. They took all the depositions, filed all the papers and scheduled a date in court. The minute Hank got drift of the D.A.'s plans to call prosecution witnesses from among Blitsky's seedier clients — payoffs, of course — Hank messengered over a confidential letter describing his witnesses from among the notorious clientele. As expected, the D.A. didn't like that one bit, nor did the mayor, nor the governor. The D.A. called offhis sleazy two-bit witnesses and now doesn't have much more than hearsay against Mike Blitsky. Try hanging a man on that.

Call Dawn.

She has been cooperative and that's been a big help. Now he's just got to see that manuscript and make sure there's nothing in there that could undermine the verdict, post-victory. He intends to earn himself wealth, power and prestige, even if it costs him his very happiness.

Do it. Dial that phone.

He lifts the receiver, closes his eyes, sends a little memo-prayer to the gods of good fortune and dials Dawn's office number.

'Dawn Waterston.'

'Hank here.'

'What's up?'

'I'm returning your call.'

'Right. Thanks. You wanted to take a look at the Blitsky manuscript? Well, we've got a draft.'

'Great. When can I get a copy? Drop by your office at six?'

'Sorry, busy. Tomorrow morning at ten?'

'Can't. Have a client. Lunch?'

'Have a meeting. After lunch, say about three?'

'No good. In court.'

'Why don't you just send a messenger, Hank?'

'I guess I could.'

'That would be the easiest.'

'In a lot of ways . . . .'

'I'll have a copy at the reception desk first thing tomorrow morning.'

'Great.'

Dawn hangs up, and Hank hangs up, and that is the end of that.

Buzz buzz buzz-

'What is it?' Hank calls back to Carla. He feels winded by that intense conversation with Dawn. At least it's over.

'Mike Blitsky called while you were on the phone. He wants you to meet him at the Royale for a drink at six. Yes or no?'

Blitsky? At the Royale? It doesn't exactly seem like his style, but if anything, the man is unpredictable.

Hank says, 'Yes,' and Carla disconnects the intercom. A phone line lights: Carla calling Blitsky back.

* * *

Tony brings Dawn her tuna on rye, carton of skim milk and granny apple, freshly delivered from the lobby deli. Then he leaves her for the sun-drenched lunchtime streets. She unwraps the sandwich. Greasy tuna is smeared on the wax paper. She lops it up with her finger, crams it back between the bread and reads *The New York Times* as she eats. She feels much better now, ever since organizing plans for this evening. It isn't exactly a date, just drinks with Blitsky at the Royale, but it's better than nothing. If she's lucky, she'll get him tipsy and come away with his initials on the changes in the manuscript and his signature on the title page. That's all she really needs to go ahead with the book. Hank thinks he's got her wrapped around his finger. He thinks she's committed to delaying the publication date. Well, she is and she isn't. She said she'd do it, and she has talked to a few people. But didn't Hank give away her engagement ring, after he'd "vowed to marry her? What's the good of a promise if you don't break it? she thinks. Her mood begins to rise, and she imagines herself as Super Editor, charging into the Royale with the manuscript bulging in her briefcase, heads turning as she dashes — Busy Executive — into the lobby to look for Mike, the oohs and ahs as she whips out her golden pen for an awed Blitsky to initial the changes and send her on her way to publishing heaven: the bestseller list. She is but a few steps away from power. Suddenly, her fantasy crashes. What is power? she desperately wonders. It's nothing but a slick penthouse with a view — to live in all alone. Dawn throws half her sandwich into the garbage and goes to the women's room to cry.

Dawn is the first to arrive at the Royale, one of her favorite places in the city to meet for an after-work drink. The lobby is a spacious, high-ceilinged room with a quaint candlelit glow. Couches and armchairs are arranged in conversation clusters around polished faux-antique coffee tables, where people meet for tea or drinks. She arranges herself in a cozy corner cluster, and orders a glass of Chardonnay.

Her cry had done her good. Now, all she wants is to get Blitsky's initials on the manuscript. She ruminates on humbled expectations, that handy rationale for complacency, when she happens to look up and ....

Hank! Here! In a panic, Dawn stands up. Should she leave before he sees her? What if he's meeting Chris? She decides she'll leave a message for Blitsky — *So sorry, but something came up* — but it's too late, Hank has spotted her.

'Dawn,' he says, almost managing to pull off a casual smile. His face, though, is bright red. 'What are you doing here?'

'Don't I have a right to be here?' she says.

Hank holds up his hands, surrender style. 'Of course you do. Sorry.' He looks around. 'I'm supposed to meet Mike Blitsky.'

'What?'

'He asked me to meet him here. Why? You, too?'

Dawn nods. 'He didn't say anything about bringing his lawyer.'

'He didn't exactly mention he was bringing his editor.'

'So.'

'Well.'

'Since we're both here, why don't you order a drink and wait with me? When he comes, we'll see what he wants. Agreed?'

'Agreed.'

Hank sits in an armchair, very obviously not joining Dawn on the couch, and orders himself a Scotch with a splash.

'Just one splash?' she quips.

'I'm feeling a little tense.'

Understandably so. Dawn is not exactly in her friendliest of moods, especially toward Hank. And why should she be nice to him? She eyes him, sipping his oily, amber Scotch, his concentration jumping around the room without focusing anywhere. Sitting across from him in this awkward silence, her anger escalates. She can't stop thinking about Hank and Chris, and how lonely she is, and her engagement ring, and how the only thing a bestseller will really do for her is get her a slightly bigger office and more work and a little extra money. Meanwhile, back in reality, she can't even give a man an erection anymore.

As Dawn recedes deeper into her private world, stocked with insecurities and resentments focused on the very man sitting so close she could reach out and feel him with her hand, Hank sits there in muted terror. His eyes dart around the room in desperate pursuit of any evidence of Mike Blitsky.

He arrives, finally, in a lavender caftan, trailing a long white silk scarf. His face is fully made-up with heavy base, rouge, purple eye shadow, black eyeliner, mascara and hot pink lipstick. He approaches Hank and Dawn with the unself-conscious confidence of royalty drifting through a crowd of gaping admirers.

'Hel-lo,' he says demurely, bending to kiss Hank once on both cheeks. To Dawn's surprise, Hank accepts the kisses. Then she remembers that he would do anything to placate a client.

'Darling,' Mike says, leaning forward to shake Dawn's hand.

He arranges himself in the other armchair, hails a waiter and orders a pink flamingo. Hank and Dawn trade conspiratorial glances of embarrassment.

'Thank you both for meeting me here,' he says. 'I like to think of us as a team.' Then, to Dawn, 'You understand that I wanted my attorney with me to discuss the changes in the manuscript, of course.'

'Of course.'

'We don't want to approve anything impulsively. One thing I can't afford to lose is my case.'

'Definitely not,' Hank says.

Dawn squeezes a smile out of her frustration. Why do men have to run everything their way? All she wanted were a few little initials. She turns her icy smile on Hank, and his hearty professional presence withers.

Blitsky doesn't miss a thing; his eyes move back and forth between them like a metronome. 'I see,' he says. 'Very, very interesting.'

Dawn hoists her briefcase to her lap and pulls out the manuscript. 'Here,' she says, dropping it on Blitsky's knees. 'The pages with changes are paper-clipped. Take a look.'

Blitsky folds his hands over the manuscript and grins like a bloated guru.

Hank nervously looks at his watch. 'I don't have much time,' he says (a lie). 'Gould we get on with this?'

Blitsky grins and doesn't look at the manuscript. 'I sense some sexual tension,' he says.

Dawn shakes her head in frustration. Hank clenches his lips together and turns red. Blitsky blooms into laughter.

'Well well well!' he says. 'What has been going on behind Mikey's back?'

Hank says, firmly but calmly, 'Nothing has been going on. Ms. Waterston and I simply don't see eye to eye on a few issues.'

'And besides,' Dawn says — and she's angry now — 'it's none of your business, Mike.'

'None of my business? Those are always the best.'

'My personal life is my own business, and no, I am not "on the rag"! I am a human being who happens to be a woman, and I am sick and tired of being manipulated and controlled and jilted by men!'

'Jilted?' says Blitsky. He looks at Hank.

'Dawn,' Hank says with extreme calm, 'not now.'

'Why not now?' She leans forward in her seat and glares at him. 'Why not? Who asked you here?'

'I did,' Blitsky says. He is ignored.

'This is my meeting, not yours. This is about my book.'

'*My* book,' Blitsky says.

'What gives you the right to waltz in here and oversee my book?' Dawn says. 'I wasted the best years of my life on you, Hank, and all I have to show for it is a tan line on my ring finger!'

Blitsky's eyes go straight for the finger. His penciled eyebrows arch dramatically.

Hank says, 'Please keep it down, we'll talk about it later.'

'Ha! Talk? What's there to talk about? You gave Christine my ring!'

'You didn't!' Blitsky says.

Dawn shoots him a look.

'Honey,' Blitsky says, 'I had no idea. Aren't men awful? They're all the same!'

She says, 'He gave this bitchy blonde my engagement ring!'

Blitsky takes Dawn's hand and strokes it. He looks accusingly at Hank.

Hank wilts into his chair and drains his Scotch.

'And I thought this was just going to be a boring business meeting,' Mike says.

Dawn starts to cry.

'As far as I'm concerned,' Hank says, 'this is a boring business meeting. And we're not getting anything done. I will not have my personal affairs exposed in the lobby of the Royale! I'm tired, Dawn, and believe me, I'm sick of this, too. Do you want to know why I gave your ring to Chris? Do you want to know why?'

Dawn cries harder. 'Yes! Why?'

'I'll tell you why! I'll tell you why!'

Dawn waits.

'Well?' Blitsky says. 'Why?'

Hank looks at Blitsky. He looks at Dawn. He clamps his teeth so his jaw bulges out, like a man who's really mad, when he's really just scared. He grabs his briefcase and marches out.

'Why?' Dawn wimpers. 'He didn't tell me why.'

'Shush, sweetkins,' Blitsky coos. 'He's a man, he doesn't know why he does what he does. Anyway, she probably forced it out of him. Whoever she is, she can't be as adorable as you.'

Dawn looks at Blitsky and feels a calm begin to wash over her. Her jagged breathing slows. 'Really?'

'Yes, really.'

'Mike, I'm so sorry about all that.'

'No, I'm sorry. Give me a pen.'

Dawn fishes into her briefcase and gives him a plastic ballpoint. Without even checking them, Mike initials all the changes in the manuscript. He hands it to her with a brilliant smile, and says, 'The fact is, I've always been a woman at heart.'

Twelve
Positive Thinking

'**D**avid Siedelman. David Sidel. David Slide. Slide David. Slide Dave —'

'Why don't you just go with Gary Cooper?'

David glares at Jack. 'Well, excuse me.' He stands up and takes a handful of popcorn. 'Would you mind not saying anything unless it's positive? Negative energy will destroy all the vibes I've been sending out for my success.' Jack swings his feet around and sits up on the couch.

'Could you stop thinking about your career just for one night?'

'I can't. I lost the detergent account and I have to do something. I need a part, a real part, a bread-and-butter part. I've been meditating on it all day. Now I need a new name.'

David paces the floor, trailing popcorn.

'You're blocking the TV, David. The least you could do when you invite me over to watch a movie is let me see the screen.'

David points the remote control at the VCR and stops the video. 'You're not focusing on being here with me.'

Jack shakes his head, exasperated.

'Do me a favor and call Kath.'

'I can't call Kath on a Saturday night, David. She probably has a date. I don't want her to think I don't.'

'Fine. Be depressed. I have to get some work.' David paces. 'Gary Cooper. Garth Cooper. Grant Cooper. Gannett Cooper. Gnarl . . . No. Garson Cropper. That's it! Garson Cropper!' He spins around to face Jack, who is slumped into the couch, his eyes fixed on the frozen image on the screen.

'Yo!'

Jack looks at David.

'Garson Cropper.'

'Great.'

'Phyllis.'

'What?'

'Phyllis might be free tonight. She's got a roommate, Laurie or Lauren or something.' He picks up the receiver of his Mickey Mouse phone and dials.

'Believe me,' David says, sitting at the bar of Pedro's Oasis, peering into the dense, trendy crowd through black sunglasses, 'these girls are fun. F-u-n. And cute —'

'C-u-t-e, I know.'

'Hey, lighten up, buddy.'

Jack gulps his mug of frothy draft beer. It feels like a hundred degrees in this room. This bar obviously has an air conditioning problem, unless all these horny New Age celibates are heating up the place with suppressed sexual tension. Probably every single person here has a condom on them, wrapped in plastic, yellowed and mashed from disuse. That old, hopeful condom — a rubber check to buy-intimacy-now, pay later. Jack's freedom has never seemed so bitter, now that the days of a sexual handshake are over. And so the question is how to restore machismo to the modern male? He already has the black leather jacket, the cowboy boots, and a wardrobe of denim and muted plaids. He's read *Iron John.* Yet something deeply lacks in his life, and he suspects he won't find it among the plastic palm fronds of Pedro's Oasis.

He slides off his barstool. 'David,' he says, 'I'm not into this, I'm going home.'

'You can't leave.'

'Just apologize for me, okay?'

David smiles. 'Sure, Jack.'

'I appreciate it. I'll return the favor.'

'No problem, Jack.'

David grins like a Cheshire cat, and who trusts the Cheshire cat? Jack looks around. Two women approach: one, a tall, lanky blonde; the other, a short, dumpy brunette. Both wear miniskirts, tube tops and backless high-heeled sandals, and both have hair permed like thick wire. Their bright pink smiles flash simultaneously. David waves them over.

Now Jack feels an urgency to leave. What's wrong with David, anyway, setting him up with a couple of bridge-and-tunnel girls? Jack may be a bridge-and-tunnel man himself, considering that he lives in Brooklyn, but he has Manhattan style.

'Hi girls.' David says. 'This is my friend Jack.'

'Hoy Jack,' the girls say in unison.

He says, 'Hello. Nice to meet you.'

The blonde girl's eyes crinkle up as if to smile, but she doesn't commit her lips to movement. She's almost pretty, with pale, freckled skin and light blue eyes. Hopefully she's Lauren. But, of course ....

'I'm Phyllis,' she says, 'and this is moy friend Lauren.'

The little brunette checks Jack out, her eyes travelling from his face to his legs and back up again. She doesn't smile, not even with her eyes. She has a round, solid face which she has tried unsuccessfully to sculpt into prettiness with shadows and lines of makeup. Her dark, squinty eyes give her a mean look. She stares at him as if she's the one who's disappointed, which intrigues Jack. No woman has ever turned him down. He is, after all, a man among men. And thus, he turns his brilliant sexy smile on Lauren, just for the hell of it. Her mouth twitches, but she still doesn't smile.

David relinquishes his stool to Phyllis, and Lauren scrambles onto the one Jack has abandoned. They both sigh and gaze around the room. They order gin fizzes. Jack stands with David next to the women, who chatter together. David presses himself into their conversation — a true chameleon — while Jack petrifies into driftwood and rests innocuously in place. Until, like a miracle wind, a distantly familiar voice calls: 'Jack! Wow! How are ya?'

Jack looks over, and there is Margo Zimmerman, transformed. She was always on the overweight side, which is only one of the reasons she never made it as an actress, and now she looks downright plush. Her short dark hair is neatly coiffed, gold earrings dangle by her neck, red lipstick glistens on her smile, and she looks sleek in a black jumpsuit and long pointy shoes. She carries a tequila sunrise in the grip of manicured fingers. She looks expensive. So, Margo has money now, unlike five summers ago, when she and Jack worked together on a road tour. She was a production assistant making about a hundred dollars a week, sacrificing everything to hang around the actors in the hope that a little opportunity would rub off. It never did. She was convinced the reason she couldn't get a part was because of her receding gums. Actually, Margo just couldn't act.

'Hey, Jack, what's up with you these days?'

'Working for Katz's Scenic'

'No kidding?'

'It's a lot of fun. You acting?'

Margo laughs. 'I gave that up a long time ago. I'm in casting now.'

David smiles brilliantly. 'Garson Cropper,' he says, and shoots out a hand to shake.

Margo can tell a hungry actor when she sees one. She smiles, nonetheless.

'I'm here with a friend,' she says. 'Why don't you guys join us?'

Jack hesitates — what about Phyllis and Lauren? — but David says, 'Love to!' Jack follows without argument. Phyllis and Lauren don't even appear to notice, but continue to talk, giggle and suck down their gin fizzes through the tiny mixing straws. David and Jack follow Margo through the hyperstylish throng to the other side of the barroom, where small tables line one wall.

Margo stops at a table where an attractive, auburn-haired woman in a blue-flowered minidress sits passively.

'This is my old friend, Jack, from the lean years.' The women laugh. 'And this is Garson Cropper.'

'I love your name,' the woman says.

David nods coolly.

'This is Ellen,' Margo says. Ellen smiles, especially at Jack, and he gets a little shiver in his spine. He smiles back, turning on his lightning eyes. 'Ellen works for Apple Eye TV.'

David shines so hard his facial muscles lock.

'Why do I think you're an actor?' Margo asks David.

'I've done some television,' he tells her, 'I had the lead in a series of shorts.'

Ellen leans forward. 'You were the guy in those detergent commercials. Yeah, I remember you. You were cute.'

'Well, some people don't respect the talent it takes to produce a good commercial. Actually, though, I'm changing genres. I'm breaking into film now.'

Jack chokes back laughter.

'Garson,' Margo says, 'I may have something for you. Do you have time for an audition next week?'

'I think I could fit one in,' he says. 'I'm between agents now, so you can reach me directly at this number.' He scribbles his number on a napkin for her, and she gives him her card.

'The bartender wants some money.' It is Phyllis, who has suddenly appeared at the table with Lauren at her side.

Lauren says, 'You guys asked us out. You guys gotta pay.'

David and Jack guiltily dig into their pockets and hand the girls what they have, which amounts to just under twenty dollars.

David has to walk home — but he doesn't really mind, he's full of energy, having been discovered by a casting agent out of the clear blue sky.

Jack, though, doesn't go home at all. Instead, he finds himself easily enticed into a cab with Ellen, destination unknown.

<u>*Thirteen*</u>
New Friends and Fortunes

Jack sits on Ellen's white leather couch, blowing his nose. 'This damn cold won't go away,' he moans.

'You sound like that ad.'

'I really don't feel like going out tonight.'

'But it's Saturday night. Besides, Chris will be very disappointed if we cancel. She can't wait to meet you. And you've got to meet her, she's my best friend. How do I look?' She stands in front of him with her hands on her hips and her legs spread in a V.

Barbarella, Jack thinks; she looks like an aging time-warp celluloid sex symbol. She has the height, the length and all the basic goods, but she's also got the inevitable saddlebags of real life on her thighs, and too much makeup covering a once-pretty face that's taken the beatings of thirty-six years. Thrice-weekly aerobics keeps her in pretty good shape. And she's got great hair: a curly auburn mop, with just a touch of henna. But that outfit: skin-tight black leggings, black-dyed aligator pumps, an oversized hot-pink shirt puckered with dime-sized bubbles, and gold earrings that dangle nearly to her shoulders.

Jack says, 'You look spectacular,' and wipes some dripping snot from beneath his nose.

Ellen's TriBeCa loft is an illegal sublet from an illegal subletter of a legal tenant whose lease would never stand up in court because the landlord never got a certificate of occupancy. She's lived here for over three years without ever fixing it up, since she expects to get thrown out at any time.

The walls are unpainted cinderblock, the floors are raw wood, and bare bulbs hang at even intervals from the high ceiling. To compensate for the barrenness, the place is loaded with expensive furniture: the white leather couch and matching armchair; a blue glass coffee table; a huge Oriental vase in the corner; a round glass dining table surrounded by six red leather chairs; an easel holding a hastily acquired, pre-fame Cindy Sherman photo of herself as lonely-urban-drifter; and a display of brilliant copper pots and pans (never used, she always eats out or orders in). A king-size canopy bed, draped with gauzy lavender lace, sits at the other end of the loft.

Often when Jack sleeps in that bed, he has uneasy dreams: he is afloat in a mass of cotton candy in an endless overcast sky, or stuck at the top of a mimosa tree like a helpless cat, or dialing Kath and getting the wrong number over and over again, or suffocating inside the wrong cloud.

'Summer colds are the worst,' Ellen says, sitting next to Jack and kissing his cheek. 'Is that what you're wearing to-night?' She points to his basic uniform of blue jeans and T-shirt, in this case a red one with a tiny hole above the breast pocket. Jack shrugs and Ellen shakes her head. 'Darling, you can't wear that to meet my friends. Please change.'

'Into what? It's all I have here.'

'All right,' Ellen sighs, 'we'll go to Chinatown or something.'

Jack feels sick. He feels tired. He feels like turning on the TV and spacing out. He feels like seeing Kath.

'I guess I'll shave,' he says, and drags himself to the bathroom.

Jack hears the intercom buzzer, the elevator churn up, the door screech open and sudden female chatter. The infamous Chris has arrived with her fiance. Jack is seized with an urge to escape. But this is not the movies, and there is no convenient bathroom window to flee through. So he finishes shaving, and doomed man that he is, nicks his throat. He makes his entrance with bloodied toilet paper stuck to his skin. Ellen glares at him; probably she'd rather he bled to death than embarrass her in front of her friends. Jack ignores her. He wiggles his Adam's Apple, smiles and introduces himself as, simply, Jack, a friend of Ellen's.' She doesn't like that, either. *Friend,* plain and simple, with no indication of his feelings for her, which of course is indication enough.

Chris sizes him up obviously, eyeballing him from head to toe. She's wearing a white miniskirt, a lime green sleeveless turtleneck, dangling orange earrings and fuchsia lipstick. Her hair is a metallic strawberry color. Her perfume smells like sweet spice. 'I'm Chris.' She flashes a plastic smile, and turns to her boyfriend. 'This is Hank, my fiance.' She lifts her left hand to display an emerald and diamond ring.

Hank shakes Jack's hand. He looks like a decent guy, a little wimpy maybe, but somehow too conservative for this flashy woman. He's tall and clean cut. And he's wearing jeans, too. Ha! Hank may be wearing a nice shirt, white with pale yellow stripes, but those are definitely good old dungarees on his bottom half. And sneakers. Brand new and squeaky white, yes, but sneakers all the same.

'Wanna beer?' Jack offers Hank.

'Sounds good.'

Hank follows Jack to the kitchen, leaving the women in a wild cackle of conversation. The men crack a couple of beers and move back into the central loft.

Ellen and Chris lean eagerly together on the couch, whispering with enthusiasm. Jack hears his name. He clears his throat and Hank blushes. The women's conversation abruptly halts.

'Poopsie poo,' Chris says to Hank. She pats the couch next to her and Hank sits. Jack is awed by the man's obedience, and shocked when Ellen tries the same thing with him.

'Honey sweets,' Ellen says, 'come sit with me.'

Jack sits in the matching armchair and takes a good long swig of his beer. Hank watches him carefully. After a minute, Hank inches away from Chris until he is leaning into the far end of the couch.

'So, Jack,' Hank says, 'what line are you in?'

Jack starts to answer, but before the words form on his tongue, Ellen says, 'He's in the theater.'

Hank nods and says, 'Oh?'

Jack clenches his jaw. 'You?' he asks.

'I'm an attorney.'

Jack is impressed and a little threatened. The guy looks about his age. So young, and already entrenched in a serious profession.

'In fact, I'm working on a very interesting case at the moment,' Hank begins.

'Oh, Hank,' Chris says, 'can we talk about something different for a change?'

Ellen says, 'So, Chrissy, how are your wedding plans coming along?'

Jack notices a slight flutter of Hank's eyelids, some kind of nervous reaction.

Chris beams. 'It's so much work! But worth it, I think.' She glances at Hank. 'I ordered the flowers, the tablecloths, the place settings, the band and the invitations. Now I've got to get on the ball and find myself a dress.'

'Oh, the dress!'

Jack winks at Hank, who suppresses laughter in a gargantuan yawn, which merits a quick smirk from Chris.

'Where've you looked so far?'

'Well, I've been to Kleinfeld twice, and I found a dreamy gown, but I just don't know . . . .'

'White?'

'Of course. It is my wedding day!'

'Only two months to go til the big day.'

'October 18th!'

Chris stands up. 'So anyway,' she says, twisting at the waist and gesturing as she describes the gown. 'It's satin with white lace netting, like this, with a fitted waist, like so, and a big skirt with four slips to give it size. The top's cut like this, scooping down the bust but not too far, and the sleeves are short but puffy, like so. And I found a fabulous little embroidered cap with the cutest puff of netting.'

'Oh!'

'I love the dress, but it's just,' her voice fades to a whisper, to say: 'a little pricey.'

Ellen whispers, 'How much?'

The women are practically glued together, but Jack can hear the awesome sum of thirty-five hundred dollars pass between them. He looks at Hank, who appears oblivious. Poor guy. Doesn't he see what's happening to him?

Jack belches and the women turn disgusted faces to him.

' 'Nother beer?' he asks Hank, who answers, 'Thanks.'

Jack was hoping Hank would offer to come with him, but he doesn't. So Jack escapes to the kitchen alone, and opens himself another beer, which he drinks at the counter. He has not been there two minutes when Chris comes in. She opens the refrigerator and gets a can of diet soda.

'Open this for me?' she says, handing it to him.

It must be those long fake fingernails of hers, Jack thinks, that make it impossible for her to open the can. He snaps it open and brown fizz bubbles up. He hands the can to Chris.

'Thanks.' She leans her hip against the counter, pressing her chest forward. Is she really batting her eyelashes or is it some kind of joke?

Jack swigs his beer. His eyes settle on her. He doesn't know what to say.

Chris twists at the waist to lean her elbow on the counter, giving her buttocks the best aesthetic advantage in the mini-skirt. Her tan, waxed legs shine.

'You seem like a nice guy,' she says. 'I don't know how you can stand that Ellen.'

Jack smiles, amazed; he thought they were best friends. 'Ellen's a nice girl,' he says, and shrugs.

That little shrug was a definite mistake. Jack should know that a girl like Chris recognizes all the signs of detachment. First she grins, then she gets him with her big blue eyes. Her foot slips along the floor and the tip of her white leather pump slides up his calf. A shiver shoots up Jack's spine, despite his better judgment. And he does know better than to let himself be vulnerable to a vamp like Chris. But he's a man, and a man has to do what a man must. And at this very moment — an unexpected moment for Jack — his most manly member is on the rise. Chris leans over and gives him a long, wet kiss right on the mouth. Her kiss feels cool, taunting. She tickles his groin and he nearly explodes. Then, suddenly, she pulls away. She wipes her mouth with a napkin. The diamonds sparkle on her finger. She takes a sip of her soda, winks and leaves.

Once Jack's erection dies down, and he can think clearly again, his most urgent desire is to warn Hank of impending doom. He must somehow get the message across to the poor guy that marrying this viper could be the worst mistake of his life. But how? They've only just met.

'Ja-ak!' Ellen calls.

He wipes traces of Chris's lipstick from his mouth and buries the napkin deep in the garbage.

Firecrackers sizzle in the steamy air: red, green, blue, gold and white sparkly fountains that rain from all directions. Mott Street bustles with old Chinese women buying fish and vegetables from open-air markets that spill out onto the side-walks. Chinese-American teenagers with black brush-cuts and rock 'n roll T-shirts bop along, embarrassed by the old ethnic grannies, their progenitors. Tiny moon-faced children led by thick-calved women giggle and cry.

Ellen and Chris, linked arm-in-arm, alternately duck from shooting firecrackers and turn around to wink at the men. At which man, exactly, is a mystery to Jack. For all he knows, Ellen has been coming on to Hank in private. While the confusion is slightly thrilling, there is one thing he feels sure of: he will never sleep with Chris. Even he is aware that there is no such thing as two copulating adults free from association; that once sex has been struck between two people, history is made — in hopes, in memories, in babies. Not to mention that sleeping with that snake would throw his whole karma out of whack. And he feels an affinity towards Hank, that poor hangdog.

They wait in line for forty minutes outside a popular restaurant whose review Ellen had seen in a recent *New York Magazine.* None of them questions the wisdom of this; Hank and Jack simply accept the female directive, standing aloof but obedient some ten feet away, just out of earshot.

'So, you're in the theater,' Hank says.

Jack smiles. 'I'm a carpenter. I build sets.'

'Aha. I see. Ellen?'

Jack shrugs. 'It's just a thing for now, if you know what I mean.'

'Kind of a mutual ambivalence situation?'

'Yup.'

'That's how we started.' Hank sighs. 'I don't know. My work's very important to me. My personal life, well, it seems to take its own course.'

'How did you and Chris meet?'

'Through a friend. I was engaged to someone else then, actually.' Hank sighs again.

'So, you're really gonna take the plunge this time?'

Hank shrugs. 'I've resigned myself to the risk.'

'No offense, but I hope I'm happier when — if— I ever get married.'

They laugh.

Hank digs into his pocket, pulls out a supple leather wallet and extracts a business card, which he hands to Jack. Jack reads the buff-colored card with its raised black lettering:

Henry Lowe, Jr. Dick, Lesser & Moore, Inc.
300 Park Avenue
New York, N.Y. 10016
tel (212) 489-8000
fax (212) 489-8954

Jack goes into his wallet, a black nylon billfold with velcro, and finds an old taxi receipt upon which he writes his name and number. He hands the battered receipt to Hank, who glances at it and slips it into his wallet.

Jack wonders if this is the time to tell Hank the truth about Chris. He glances casually up and down Mott Street, looks over at the women — who are huddled together, giggling and whispering — and says, 'Actually, I've been thinking. I wonder if maybe this wed . . . .'

'Oh goodie!' Chris says. 'Come on, guys, our table's ready.'

Jack looks at Hank and shrugs. Hank shrugs back.

The foursome are seated at a rectangular table with packets of salt, pepper, sugar and sugar substitute, a red plastic ashtray and a bottle of soy sauce crammed into the center. Ellen smiles at Jack. Chris pats Hank's arm. Chris's foot rubs Jack's leg. And who knows what's going on under the table between Ellen and Hank.

And who really cares? The sorry truth of the matter is that these are couples that are not meant to be, at least not in the ultimate scheme of things. But how will it all be resolved? How will the sword of truth come to separate them from each other, and doom? Well, truth comes in many shapes and colors. Even, sometimes, in a fortune cookie.

At the end of the meal they are served a plate of orange slices and fortune cookies. They pluck their cookies from the plate at random, and here is how it reads:

Chris: *Gems are but stones, love is the real bounty.*
Hank: *Look not askew for your worst enemy, but into your own heart and home.*
Ellen: *Every thoroughbred is half a horse's ass.*
Jack: *Never turn your back from true love, or it will escape you when you're not looking.*

Fourteen
Peculiar Politics

Kath and Andy sit across from each other at a cozy table, with a stumpy yellow candle flickering between them. It may not be love but it passes the time. Fishy Waters, Andy's favorite Cajun restaurant, is a cavernous white stucco room decked out in nautical motif: fish plaques, heavy nets draped in the corners, glowing yellow lanterns perched on the walls and a huge wooden wheel studded with electric flames hanging in the center of the room. It's Saturday night and Kath is glad to be out at a real restaurant, a change from simple, wholesome meals alone or take-out Chinese at Dawn's. She's wearing Dawn's madras sundress and feels just like a regular woman out on a regular date. This is the first time she's been out with Andy that she hasn't felt cheated by wishing she were out with Jack instead. In fact, she is enjoying herself; Andy is charming in his own peculiar way.

What Kath can't understand is why he puts up with her. They've been seeing each other for six weeks, and he seems eager to please her, yet she is flagrantly casual with him. She goes out with him only when it's convenient for her and she cancels if something better comes up. Sometimes she sleeps with him, sometimes she doesn't, and it's never hotter than lukewarm. Andy's a smart man, doesn't he realize he's being used? Doesn't he want more out of life? So she asks him, point-blank (after all, she has no emotional stake in his answer, or so she thinks): 'Have you ever considered a more serious involvement?'

Andy slowly sips his vodka. 'I have to be honest with you, Kath, because I like you. The truth is, I'm not ready for a serious commitment with one woman now. I have a stable of women, and though I cherish you especially, I'm just not ready to be a one-woman man yet. Sorry.'

Kath is stunned and embarrassed. She had felt that she was doing him a favor by dating him at all. To think that Andy Shoemaker, *homo unerect,* is a womanizer after all.

To her surprise, Kath finds herself subject to pangs of jealousy over Andy's other women. The thought of his warm pudgy body rolling over someone else's the night before or the night after their own times together disturbs her. With Jack, knowledge of other women is a deep, persistent despair. With Andy she simply wishes she didn't know because it changes the tenor of their relationship. His confession has shifted the balance of power; the ball that has dribbled so faithfully in her court, is now bouncing around his.

But worse than mere craziness and chaos is danger — is AIDS. Promiscuity now is like courting death, and here she has let it into her life, again, through Andy Shoemaker, the chubby dull man who can barely get hard.

Fishy waters, indeed.

As a cloud of depression hovers by, as she feels its cold shadow overtake her, Kath's mind turns to the ending of this madness. She hates the ambiguity, the confusion, the lack of real connection. There is nothing fulfilling about playing musical beds, except that it gives her Jack now and then. Or does it, really? She is distressed to recognize an affinity between her life now and her field of study, a relation she had made with fascination between Mike Blitsky's life and the eighteenth century novel, a schema of the politics of love, bawdy and picaresque and in the end downright ridiculous. The players barter for marriage partners among those who are suitable, desirable and better yet, rich. They want love, one way or another; most want money; all want both. A few get what they want, and others end with a shoddy bargain that they resolve to live with. Yet they all play by the spoken and the unspoken rules with a sharp spirit of competition. And they all play to win, even if the odds are against them.

Kath bemoans the connection she makes between then and now. Why can't she just have Jack? Why won't he just have her? Submit to love, body and soul? Sexually they do submit, albeit with condoms in this late twentieth century madness. But emotionally they are players, bartering, cheating, compromising for a better eventual win. All they are really doing though is losing out. It's a crazy, senseless game, played with skill, with losses checked against the larger unrealized balance. Where had they learned the rules?

From the eighteenth century. From the myth of the apple and the snake.

Sexuality has always been analyzed, challenged, feared and celebrated; and now, it has become the vehicle for plague. No amount of confusion can cloud the fatal fact of AIDS. Kath is angry that Hank slept with Chris before he broke up with Dawn, and she is angry that Jack needs other women, and she is angry that even Andy, whom she had thought safe, has dragged her into his 'stable'. She is angry at these men, and deeply saddened, and exhausted, and finally decides to finish with the games. She'd rather be alone with Dr. Johnson and her books than tied up in this crazy knot with faithless men whose roaming confusion could bring her beyond mere heartbreak, to death's door.

Kath gazes around the library at the rows of books: each a treasure of thought and passion and history and wisdom; each a testament to human frailty and the will to overcome ignorance and pain. She knows that she ultimately became a scholar to give shape to her search for definition, understanding, inner peace. It has always been through reading that she found solace, and through writing that she was able to articulate her confusion and locate solutions. She raises the screen of her laptop, lifts her fingers to the keys and stares into the blank rectangle of the LED in the top left corner of which a tiny triangular cursor pulses, waiting for direction.

Peculiar Politics

Had I more fully suspected the inward bent of Michael's mind, I would have said, instead of yes, *perhaps*. Yet even now, as I write, I further retreat; for *perhaps* please substitute *no.*

Upon consideration and reconsideration of the peculiar politics which moved our every meeting forward, what must be admitted to, Sir, is a lack of the great uniter of souls. That strange, ephemeral power which joins first the eyes, then hearts, then hands. I repulse at naming it, you know what it is; that word so rife with illusion and, yes, inequity. Upon having first conceived that *word,* that great uniter, as, perhaps, applying to us, I became aghast with fear and remorse at its impossibility. From that moment onward, aware of the not so quaint directionlessness of our each and every meeting, I openly flicked the switch of the motor that was to be our constant drive.

The motor of which I speak would be, of course, the great battle of wills in which man and woman, with such vigor, and perhaps of necessity, engage. I gave myself freely to it — with what horror I admit this! And Michael, what thought he? In his eyes I read pleasure, yes, and some concern.

'So beautiful,' said he, 'that face.'

'Aha!' rebutted I, 'and so it is my face you enjoy, not what lies behind it.' At which his hand ran from shoulder to back to leg. Had our first meeting been so similar, so horizontal, all would now, I think, fall more smoothly into place. But the very verticality of our original debates forced me to focus still upon their intent. 'No! No! You must understand me,' cried I. 'Without a deeper meaning we are not to be. It must not be. It cannot be!'

'Time heals all wounds,' were his presumably soothing words then. 'In time you will certainly come around and see my meaning, and trust it together with me.'

'You speak of trust?' *He* spoke of trust! 'Where, my friend, if indeed I may call you that, lies this trust of which you speak with such seemingly heartfelt belief?' Here Michael's smile grew lewd and rakish; I cannot go on, yet I must. 'I was a fool to agree to your proposal,' said I, turning my back to him. 'A complete and utter fool.'

'You looked not foolish ten minutes ago,' said he in a voice intended to melt. A slight smile crept onto my face, yes, but I hastened to conceal it, and successfully I must admit.

'How long have we known one another?' mused I aloud, then ventured to supply the answer myself: 'Too long I think.'

'Not nearly long enough,' said he, leaping up. He plucked from the floor a very green pair of shorts, and thus, so scantily attired, set upon his rowing machine. I could not bear to watch the flex of muscle and ripple of fat, yes, the very accumulation of sweat upon his forehead.

Full of resentment at his protestations at my protestations, I dragged with me the bedsheet and, in his living room, discovered a needed silence. Upon my soul, thought I, this man so begs me to remain. Yet his behavior is so vexing. I quickly recalled the laughter upon the clinking of our glasses; his subtle smile upon signing the credit card receipt; his boyish frown upon my deliberate 'good night'; his sweet admission of *potential* devotion. Both Michael and the night proved equal to the task; yet morning is a great disclaimer! Heavy headed and clear eyed, one may now see one's true position. For that man, in the company of his avowed *potential beloved*, heartily rowed the morning away.

Alone for days after, the picture became quite clear. A female is wise to counter always 'please' with 'perhaps', and leave her seducer alone, yet with a sensation of having not half lost, but half won. She is wise to create in her seducer a sense of time and continuation, of slow, steady gain, which, in the end, will leave him acquired not only of a conquest but of an attachment as well. Thus and only thus will she wisely create for herself a steady friend, while her lover has found his own pleasant lover, and one, furthermore, of which he has grown too persuaded to discard.

A long procession of days passed, unattended by any form of invitation from Michael. My heart did sink; I had moved wrongly against myself; I had realized my own advice too late. Yet inch by inch remorse replaced itself with a steady, though shallow, detestation. Never again, vowed I, would I hear the voice of that man, and I was truly glad of it.

The very shallowness of my resolve became revealed to me upon the very next day after its heartfelt conception. For Michael called me then. Nearly one complete week had passed. Yet I said nothing of it; my reception was cool. Was I 'free' this night? asked he. 'Perhaps,' said I, with a yawn. 'Let me consult my calendar.' I allowed one minute to pass on the clock before replacing the receiver to my ear. 'It seems,' said I casually, 'that something could be possible for this evening, indeed.' In a rush, I dressed, thinking: at last he has called! I found myself quite ready to forgive. But forget, I would learn, I could not.

We met at a not fine but adequate restaurant, where the food was modest, and the prices even more so. The one great expense of the meal was laid upon the wine, of which, it seemed, we consumed nearly two bottles. Wine will work a different, deeper night upon the mind than that which blinds the eye. Benumbed and quite betricked, I willingly allowed this man, who appeared to my confused perceptions a prince, to remove me to his neighborhood in a rented yellow chariot.

Come morning, that great revealer, thought I: I will never marry Michael, even should he ask! My removal from his potential affections I took care to exhibit to him as often as possible. Carelessly did I return the towel to the rack; artlessly did I stir my coffee; casually did I note the late morning hour and the necessity of our parting ways; directly did I leave. Yet, despite my efforts, Michael appeared barely moved. I would have to more distinctly pronounce my resolution of detachment.

Fresh was this resolution in my mind when, but three days later, Michael called me. I was quite prepared to find myself indisposed at his offering of an invitation; but my plan was dashed upon his admission that, much as he 'would like' to see me, he would be quite 'tied up' for nearly two weeks, and had called only to 'check in'.

'Perhaps,' said I, 'another time.' And perhaps, indeed, I meant.

Three weeks it was before I received his call, full of excuses and declarations of having missed and wanted me night after night.

'Let us,' said I, 'then meet this Sunday afternoon,' thinking to put his affection for me to the test during the clarity of daylight. Michael promptly agreed, which seemed a good sign.

I awoke early on Sunday to put some chores out of the way, thus freeing up the remainder of the day for my appointment. The hour of meeting was to be two o'clock. Come one o'clock, however, the ring of the telephone quite broke the flow of my activities and utterly undid my plan. Michael explained that unexpected duties had forced him to the office, and begged me to meet him later that evening for a meal. What was I to do? The man was well aware of my availability that day and night, for I had already assigned the time to him. I said yes, meaning perhaps, and intending, now, to deliver a firm no the next time such an incident occurred.

Not long did I have to wait for Michael to snatch the rug from beneath my feet. I was still his one and his only potential true love; this he told me repeatedly. Yet, as I looked back over the weeks, even months, of our otherwise casual acquaintanceship, I found that never had I known this man in the day that I had not been with him the previous night. The notion of our meeting in daylight became nothing less than an obsession and I was bent, nay, determined in that direction. Toward that end, I became quite busy each night of the week, and quite available on Saturday afternoon. Michael, with pleasure, said he, agreed to an afternoon's stroll through Central Park. Once again, I arose early to complete my household chores and duties; and once again, Michael caused my phone to ring with a last minute excuse, and an invitation for the night.

'Absolutely not!' cried I, quite meaning it. Such use, such abuse, I could tolerate no more. The recklessness of our attachment had made the ties that bound us too thin to hold us together even one day longer. 'Good bye, Michael, and good luck,' I lied, for I wished the man nothing but future disaster.

He will call again, thought I, and ask my forgiveness; I will not give it at first; I will let him beg; and then, perhaps, in time, I will yield.

Days passed, then weeks, and weeks again. Michael, it seemed, had been too conscious of the easy terminability of our attachment, if attachment it can be called.

And so to all I say: begin on the winning side, and counter your opponent's sweet promises and tender entreaties with a firm, yet not quite promising, *no.* From there, I suspect, he will be all acquiescence, and you dear lady, quite the happier for it.

* * *

Answers rise to the surface of the page — the screen. She feels somewhat that she has wasted an afternoon of research on a ditty of questionable quality that will stay locked in the chips of her hard drive forever. But she also feels that writing this story has helped her to define her next step, and that her new resolution to unclog the romantic mess will free her to move on and concentrate on her real work. So what feels like a few wasted hours is probably the most valuable way she could have spent her time.

Resolved, she calls Andy late that night. His voice sounds groggy, as if he has been asleep.

'I've been reading,' he says.

'I've been thinking,' she says.

'Yes?'

'I can't see you.'

'Of course you can't see me, we're on the phone.'

'No, I can't see you anymore.'

Silence.

'You can rent out my stall to someone else.'

'Oh,' he says. 'I understand.'

She imagines him sitting on his bed in his red robe, poring over his calendar. Like a cartoon, a bubble swimming with women's names is suspended above his head. One of the names slides through his brain, through his arm and his pen and into Kath's slot.

Next, she phones Jack. His machine answers; he's probably out with one of *his* other girlfriends. She leaves a message: 'Hi, it's Kath. I'm calling to cancel our date for tomorrow. And please don't call me again, Jack. I'm not interested in this arrangement anymore.'

She takes a deep breath, lets out some air. Then it hits her: she had named the anti-hero of her story Michael, like Mike, as in Blitsky; Michael to portray Andy. Only now does it strike her how much they look alike.

Fifteen
Next Time is Now

That Chris — nothing but wine in the house, when she knows he likes beer. Ever since she started planning the wedding, she has forgotten all about him; she's always out shopping or on the phone with one of her girlfriends. And the bills! You'd think she was royalty, the way she's spending:

Engraved invitations (Tiffany)	$847
Loft rental	$2,500
Catering: hors d'oeurves and dinner for two hundred	$6,000
Place settings (rented)	$950
Floral centerpieces	$1,500
Misc. flower arrangements	$1,000
Full bar and service	$2,000
Cake	$500
Band	$1,000
Dress	$4,250
Hat w/veil	$600
Shoes	$300
Misc. tips	$500
Misc. taxes	$500
Misc. miscellaneous	$1,000
ESTIMATED TOTAL:	**$23,447**

Hank's heart races when the estimated total of Chris's wedding blinks on the calculator. He finishes his wine and pours another glass. He needs to numb his brain, and fast. This wedding will sink him deep into debt for years. It's ludicrous to spend so much on a party. That's all it will be: an overdone fashion show for Chris and her friends, with Hank just a mannequin in a tuxedo. As for the old tradition of the bride's family paying for the wedding, Chris claims that her parents never liked her and she just couldn't ask them to help. Hank doesn't like her much either at this moment, and as the calculator's LED reveals to his mind's eye the cipher of his inevitable doom, he is struck with terror at what he has let himself slip into. He has a dark vision of their future: he will work day and night and feed tons of money into the hungry machine of their life, then he'll be snuffed out by a sudden heart attack and die, leaving her a hefty life insurance policy and pension to live on; she'll get chunky and wear tight clothes, spend her days having facials and manicures, and spend his money on high fashion and expensive trips.

Where is she? It's after nine o'clock. Did she come home to be with him, to feed him? Did she even call to tell him where she is? No!

Questions surface in a rapid-fire of cerebral openings, linking him suddenly with a deeper level of emotional thought than he is accustomed to entertaining. He now wonders if his attachment to Chris is based more on low self-esteem than actual love. After all, when he breaks it down, he can see that he's handsome, he's smart, he's a rising star in his law firm, he does his chores (and let's face it, hers too), he calls to say he'll be late, he buys costly gifts. Why would he choose her over Dawn? Why is he more comfortable with a woman who treats him like dirt, than one to whom he is gold? His mind swims in anger and pain and confusion and alcohol. He can feel the liquid drug flipping switches in his brain, breaking dams, drowning him in clarity.

Nine-thirty. She's done this before.

Last time, it was with some guy from her office. 'Politics,' she said when she came home at nearly two a.m. A drink or two, maybe some dinner. That was all right, Hank could forgive that. But still, she should have called. She had promised to call 'next time.'

An hour later, still no call.

O! misery. Hank knows he's a fool. He saw the way Ellen's new boyfriend, Jack, was looking at him, wondering why he was letting Chris push him around. Why did he ever get involved with Chris? Agree to marry her? He remembers the last time she pulled this stunt. Then, as now, he paced furiously and got blazing drunk. He waited, feeling confined and suffocated. He vowed that 'next time' this happened, he would leave, end it.

Well, *next time is now.*

It only takes twenty minutes to pack: three suits, five shirts, four ties, five pairs of boxer shorts, five undershirts, five pairs of socks, one pair of jeans, two T-shirts, leather shoes, (he's wearing his sneakers), razor, shaving cream, cologne, dandruff shampoo, and the green and black checkered toothbrush that Dawn bought him just before he left her.

Can he ever hope to get her back? *Probably not,* he thinks, spiralling deeper into the nether region of his doom. He pauses, momentarily frozen in despair, and then jolts toward the bath-room where he splashes his face with cold water. He looks at himself staring back in the mirror and sees a man resolved on action. No more passive waiting, no more getting stepped on, no more swallowing doubts and frustration. Hank is a man on the move, a man with a mission, a man with his suitcase packed and ... nowhere to go.

He sighs, sits down and pours himself another glass of wine. He doesn't want to call Andy, whom he feels he can't trust. He won't call anyone from work. Then it strikes him: there is one person he knows won't have judged him through all this; one person he feels he can really trust, who may agree to harbor him.

Hank climbs the dark staircase, clutching his suitcase, his suit-bag slung over his shoulder. He can hear the occasional crunch of a roach underfoot. To think of how far he has come, materially speaking, while she still lives here: ethical, earthy and true.

The door is open a crack and a pair of yellow eyes peer out at him. It's been so long since he has been here, he has actually forgotten about Dr. Johnson. He can't even remember when he last saw Kath.

She is lying on the couch, reading a book, calmly waiting, just like old times. He stands in the doorway and looks at her, takes in the familiar scene. Then he notices her hair — where did it all go?

She twists around and smiles.

'You shouldn't leave your door unlocked,' he says, closing the door behind him.

He knows that everyone reprimands her for this unsafe habit, that she never listened before and won't now. One of the many things Hank always liked about Kath was her obstinance. She does and lives exactly as she wants, without compromise. But now, he wonders, at thirty, isn't her life a little lonely?

'You look kind of cute like this.' He grazes her punky hair with the palm of his hand.

'It was an impulse,' she says. 'Put your suitcase down anywhere. It's good to see you. I'm glad you called me.'

Hank puts his bags in a corner, and they sit together on the couch.

'You don't have to tell me what happened,' she says, 'unless you feel like talking.'

He does want to talk to her — he trusts her — but how much should he reveal? If he tells Kath how miserable his life with Chris is, won't he look like a total fool? What if he decides to go back? He looks at his knees. He's still wearing the pants he wore to work: chocolate brown lightweight wool. 'There's a lot of pressure lately with the wedding plans,' he says. Kath nods. 'And work,' he says. 'The case I'm working on right now is coming to a head.'

'I know. I did some research for Dawn.'

Hank looks at her. 'It's no secret. It was paid work. I took a little trip to Bayonne.'

'Ah, Bayonne.' He smiles just slightly. 'So, you're the crack investigator.'

'I had a little help from the cook.'

'What?'

'It's a long story. Anyway, Hank, you'll win the case and Dawn will have her big book and everyone will be happy. And you'll marry Chris.'

Happy. Was that the word she used? Happy?

'I don't know, Kath, I just don't know.' He shakes his head. He wants to open up to her, to let her wisdom guide him, to allow her to be his real friend. 'What's your honest opinion of all this?'

'You really want to know?'

'Yes, I do.'

'Okay, here goes. I don't understand what you're doing. I mean, my head understands, but my heart doesn't. I don't know Chris, so I don't know what you have with her. But I do know Dawn. She's still in love with you, Hank.' His nerves jump. 'But I think you know that,' she says. 'This career stuff, well . . .' She shrugs. 'Everyone's into their own thing. I guess I've buried myself neck-deep in my work. But I wouldn't give up love if I had it. Though I realize a lot of people do.' She stops abruptly. 'I don't mean to lecture you.'

'No,' he says, 'you're right. I've made some errors in judgment. Now, though, I'm kind of stuck.'

'So, how long do you think you want to stay? You don't have to decide, or commit. . .'

The C word — and she's laughing.

'Will I be intruding if I stay a couple nights? I'd like to have a day or two to think things through.'

'No problem.'

He wants to ask her if she has someone. But he can't. What if she misunderstands his interest? He could see himself falling for her . . . but instantly stops such a dangerous thought. Kath is an appealing woman, attractive, smart, a good listener. It would be too easy to have an affair with her. Just think of the ramifications of that: there's Dawn; there's the possibility that it wouldn't work out anyway; and then there's Chris (another nasty C word). No, don't drag Kath into this. Be a man, control yourself. He crosses his legs and hoists Dr. Johnson onto his lap.

'Would you like something, Hank? Coffee or tea? Juice? A beer?'

'A beer,' he says.

'I think I have some German beer. I remember you used to like that, right?' She disappears briefly and returns with a cold green bottle of beer. 'No clean glasses,' she says.

He drinks from the bottle, feeling a carbonated swish in his stomach as the beer hits all that wine. Kath sits at the table with a glass of ice water.

'Listen, Kath, there's one special request. I think it would be best if you didn't tell Dawn I'm here. It would only upset her and I don't know what I'm going to do yet.'

Her steady eyes unnerve him. Finally, she nods. 'Okay. But she calls me, you know. Better not answer the phone.'

'I probably won't be around much, anyway. I have a lot of work to do at the office.'

But Hank can barely concentrate on his work. All the next day, he sits there, trying to force a rational decision about his life, spinning himself into a tangle. Desperate, he decides to seek advice.

He buzzes Carla. 'Could you come in here, please?'

She walks into his office with a pad of paper and a pen, wearing a loose yellow skirt and a black sleeveless sweater, and looks, he thinks, uncharacteristically pretty. He notices a trace of lipstick on her mouth. She is chewing gum.

'Please close the door.'

She does so, and then sits in the chair in front of his desk.

'Carla,' he says. He pauses, places his fingertips together in a steeple, looks at the ceiling. 'Carla,' he says again.

'Yeah?'

'If you were a woman, and I were a man . . .'

'I am a woman and you are a man.'

'What I mean is, if you and I were a man and woman together, so to speak, and we were, let's say, quite close, and had, in fact, made a commitment of sorts, and you, for instance, were very excited about, say, getting married, but I, for example, had some grave doubts, how would you feel, hypothetically, if I requested a possible postponement of the, shall we say, commitment?'

Carla removes the gum from her mouth and sticks the little ball to her pad. 'You don't want to marry Chris,' she says. 'I can't say I'm surprised.'

'I am simply hypothesizing.'

'Alright. X wants to get married. Y doesn't. I think Y has got to tell X and get it over with.'

'Just tell her?'

'End it fast and clean, you'll be better off, and you'll get over it.'

'Y may have a difficult time explaining.' He leans forward on his elbows. 'And X, well, X won't take it sitting down.'

'Well, then just get married.' She shrugs.

'Just get married? That would certainly be the easiest thing for Y to do.'

'So, what about D? Is Y thinking about calling D?'

'Possibly.'

'Well, they say you shouldn't give advice, but just in case you want some, C thinks Y should dump X and call D.'

Yes, Hank thinks, yes. That would be the thing to do.

Bear up, be brave, have courage, and break up with Chris before more time races by, and more expenses. Maybe Dawn will forgive him. And even if she doesn't, he'll be better off without Chris.

'Thank you, Carla. You're a gem.'

'No charge.'

She starts to leave, when suddenly Hank remembers: 'Oh, Carla! What about the ring?'

She stops and thinks a moment. 'Better let her keep it, sort of like a consolation prize, you know? You can get D a different, nicer ring. It'll be expensive, but Hank, face it, you fucked up big time.'

And so are great decisions made. Hank is resolute and knows just what to do: break up with Chris; find a long-term temporary place to live; see if Dawn will have him back; and, if she will, move back in with her; or, if she won't, buy a co-op at the current low prices, wait a few years for the economy to rebound, then cash in.

'I think you're on the right track,' Kath says, when he explains his plan of action. She takes a sip of beer and sets it back down on the coffee table, which is littered with mail and newspapers. 'I'd let you stay here if there were more room.'

'I appreciate it. You've been terrific'

'What are friends for?'

Impulsively, he rubs her knee, then quickly withdraws his hand. 'Sorry,' he mumbles.

'That's okay.'

And, by the sound of her voice, it was okay. Does she want it, too? But they can't, they mustn't, they would be fools to pursue this thread of attraction.

'It's not that I'm not attracted to you,' he says. He just has to tell her. Poor Kath, always so alone. He wishes he were in a position to fall in love with her, if only it weren't so politically wrong.

'I know,' she says with surprising confidence. 'I've had nothing but bad bets lately. There was someone, but it's over.'

'Serious?'

'For me. And I think for him, too.'

'I'm sorry.'

Her eyes go deep and sad.

'When I'm settled somewhere, we can see movies together, go out to dinner, keep each other company. Maybe it'll even be like old times, you and Dawn and me.'

She smiles, but without spirit. She was always the third wheel. Hank and Dawn loved having her with them, but it was easy to tell that she was uncomfortable at times.

Kath goes with Hank to look at rental rooms in the neighborhood, and they find one nearby. It's just a small maid's room in the back of a large apartment, but it has a private bath and kitchen privileges. He moves in that very night, and as he settles in, he discovers that he has forgotten his toothbrush. He almost goes back to Kath's to get it, but decides not to. He came so close to kissing her. Too much temptation could wear him down, especially now, in his vulnerable state.

He has got to move forward, get strong, take care of business. He has got to confront Chris. But the more he thinks about it, the more panicked he becomes. She'll pulverize him. He won't be able to get away. She'll drag him down to City Hall and marry him before he knows what hit him.

He finally accepts that he will not go see her, despite intentions, and so he'll have to write a letter. On a crisp piece of Dick, Lesser & Moore letterhead, he writes:

Dear Christine:

In writing this letter, I feel compelled to be honest not only with you but with myself. It is all too clear to me that we are not, ultimately, compatible; that we hold different values; and that our emotional requirements are not mutually complementary. Please cancel all wedding plans and get a refund of deposits, where applicable. Send the checks to me at the address above.

As for the engagement ring, I ask you to graciously accept it as a token of my good faith.
Warmly, Hank

He has Carla send the letter by certified mail, return receipt. After a week or so to let things settle, he'll call Dawn.

Sixteen
The Telltale Toothbrush

Noise! Dawn slams shut her office door. Muffled noise. She presses her hands to her ears, but it's no use; she can't block the world out of her consciousness. Her hands fall to her lap and her fingers entwine. Maybe she should take up yoga? Meditation? Something to ease her battered nerves. She briefly considers revisiting her old therapist, and quickly discounts it as time consuming, expensive, and a challenge beyond her patience these days. She realizes the irony in that to return to therapy she would need to calm down first, like straightening up because the housekeeper's coming. That she never wanted her therapist to see her weaknesses impeded her growth in that quiet room; when he spotted them and described them back to her, it only made her mad. She closes her eyes and tries to clear her mind of all thought, but it doesn't work. Her brain sizzles. She hears a sharp rapping sound.

Her eyes snap open. It's real: someone is knocking on her office door.

'It's open,' she says.

A brown suede shoe toes its way in.

She says, 'Ha ha, very cute.'

Fingers curl around the edge of the door. A head of thick brown hair appears, followed by a smile, a straight nose and hazel eyes.

'Hello, Gregg.'

He stands there waiting for an invitation to sit down, but she doesn't ask him in. Resistance is the name of this game.

Gregg Badley has a goal, to further their sensual exploration of each other. So far, they have kissed three times, all unpremeditated, stolen moments: after an innocent long lunch at which the attraction first flared; late one evening in her office; and during a chance meeting in the elevator, on the way up to the office. But Dawn has decided, without a doubt, that it will never go beyond this. He shuts the door and says, 'Dawn —'

'We already went through it, Gregg.'

She stands up and walks to the window. A lunchtime crowd flows through wavering late-summer heat. The sky is blue and cloudless, light, carefree — the wrong kind of weather to turn away romance.

Gregg comes up from behind and embraces her. She hasn't been held in a long time and her body automatically melts at the warmth of human touch. It isn't Gregg, she reminds herself; it could be anyone. She runs a finger along his hands, which are clasped around her waist.

'Where is it?' she asks, and turns to face him.

He looks into her eyes like a lover but she knows he's only weighing odds. Gregg is the director of subsidiary rights; he negotiates terms and percentages for a living. He makes good deals for the company and he makes good deals for himself. The man is quicksand. She knows she's coming too close and could lose her footing. He smiles, shrugs, thrusts his hands into his pants pockets. Then, presto, one hand reappears in a fist. His fingers slowly open. A gold band sits in the middle of his palm, shining.

'Put it on,' she says sharply.

He slides the wedding band onto his ring finger.

'Now Gregg,' she says, stepping up to him and gently touching his face. 'You are very married. I am very single. This will not work.'

'Yes it will.'

'Put it this way: it won't work for *me*.'

He reaches out and pulls her to him. He moves her hair away from her neck and bends to kiss her. Dawn grabs his tie and pushes up the knot. He chokes and backs off.

'Okay?' she says.

Loosening his tie, he answers, 'No, it is not okay. Dawn, I really feel for you.'

Oh, how she wants to hear that, from him or anyone. She's so lonely, she needs someone to love her, someone to love. But not Gregg.

'I feel sorry for your wife,' she says.

'Little Miss Morality.'

'Try Big Mr. Unethical. I wouldn't want to be your wife.'

'No threat of that.' He pokes forward his squarish chin, straightens his tie and leaves.

Dawn locks her office door. Seconds later, the persistent knocking starts again. He won't stop, he just won't let this go. What if one of their colleagues sees this ridiculous episode? She presses her palms to her ears, squeezes shut her eyes and wishes he would stop.

'Honey, are you in there?' says an artificially high male voice.

Dawn bolts to her desk to check her appointment book, which is open to yesterday; she's so distracted, she hasn't even checked today's schedule. She flips the page and there it is: Mike Blitsky, ten o'clock, here.

She unlocks the door. 'Mike, I'm so sorry. Please come in. Please forgive me.'

'Forgiven,' he says cheerfully. He kisses her cheek and sits down, smoothing the tops of his grey silk slacks. The matching double-breasted jacket appears to have shoulder pads.

'I caught you on the Letterman show,' Dawn says.

'Was I good?' He smiles that big, proud, gap-toothed smile of his.

'You were terrific'

He reaches into his pink plastic shoulder bag and hauls out a draft of the manuscript.

'Who,' he says, 'has been to Bayonne?'

'But Mike, you already signed off on that chapter.'

'You had me bewitched. I should have read it then and there, but I didn't.'

The fact is, and Dawn knows it, that she got his initials in a few places and that a contract does not make.

'Tell me just what the problem is,' she says.

'My family isn't exactly proud of me. Both my mothers are dead so they won't mind, and my father's gone so incognito that even I don't know where he is. It's my brothers I'm worried about. Oh, what creeps they were! I haven't seen them in years and that's fine with me. We never got along, they always poopooed me.' He leans forward and raises his inky eyebrows. 'I'm afraid of a lawsuit from one of them, or both of them. It could be libelous to write about my brothers at all, and if I were you, Dawn, I'd be careful. We'd all be better off if you just scrapped any mention of them.'

'Do you know where they are now?' Dawn asks. She thinks of Marco — Blitsky's half-brother — and wonders if she should tell Mike. That awful Marco! For all his effort to fit the status quo, she likes Mike so much more with his flagrant amorality and flashy clothes. No, she won't tell him about Marco. Anyway, she never found out where he lives.

'My roots, darling Dawn, have dissolved,' Mike says wistfully.'What people really want is the dirt. And it's all here, from my first trick to the building up of my illustrious and shocking clientele.' He smiles. 'That's what people want. Not a lot of dribble about sibling rivalry.'

'Okay, Mike. I'll edit your brothers out except for one brief mention. You won't challenge the rest of the childhood chapter?'

Mike pouts his lips. His made-up eyes blink. He smiles. 'No. For you, anything.'

'Thanks. Then we're agreed. We've moved the pub date to right after your trial. Will that be a problem?'

'Better ask my lawyer,' he says.

'Right.'

'Speaking of which — how's the love life?'

Dawn rolls her eyes and shakes her head. 'Not good.'

'Tell all, Dawn, who was that enticing man sulking by your door when I came in?'

'That enticing *married* man, you mean?'

'Aha, I see.'

'So that's that.'

'I suppose you've met the wife.'

'Of course not!'

Mike wags his finger in the air. 'Now don't give this one up until you've met the wife. She is always the key in these affairs. Until you've seen her, you do not know what you're dealing with. Take it from Misled Mike, I speak from experience. I've had the honor of breaking up a few marriages myself. Married men cannot resist me, or most of my Marvelous Men, for that matter.'

'I don't know, Mike. I've always vowed I would never get involved with a married man. Maybe I am a moralist, maybe I'm a prude, maybe I'm scared, but I want a man of my own.'

'Of course you do, dear. My point is simply that, until you've met the wife, you can only guess whether you can get that man for yourself, or not. It might not be a lost cause. After all, some single men are harder to catch.'

How true! Take Hank, she thinks ....

'Trust me, sweetheart. Meet her.'

Dawn is in turmoil for the rest of the day. Could Mike be right? There's an office party coming up and Gregg's wife might be there. Dawn could do it; she could walk in, saunter right up and innocently introduce herself. But then, Dawn thinks, how could she even consider making off with another woman's husband? Particularly since she lost her own true love to the wiles of an unscrupulous other woman. No, she decides, this is one heartbreak she must avoid bestowing and receiving. But even at the moment of resolve, she is aware that such rigid determination is often a sign of weakness.

* * *

Dawn sees Dr. Johnson sitting sphinx-like on the windowsill and feels instantly comforted. She hurries around the corner and waits impatiently for Kath to buzz her in. Then she bounds up the steps to Kath's landing, where Dr. Johnson has meanwhile taken his post at the open door. Dawn bends to scoop him up. He struggles out of her grip and dashes into the bedroom.

Kath sits at her table of books by the open window, wearing gym shorts and a tank top. 'I wish I had a cross breeze,' she says. She takes a cube of watermelon from a large ceramic bowl, pops it into her mouth and lifts a cupped palm to catch the seeds. She rapidly spits out four, and says to Dawn, 'Have some watermelon.'

Dawn shuts and locks the door, sheds as much clothing as possible —jacket, shoes, belt, bracelet — and sits at the table with her friend. She puts a cube of watermelon into her mouth, and the sweet watery taste gives her a quick recollection of lazy summer vacations, swinging on ropes from big trees, jumping naked into warm, placid lakes. She looks at Kath, who appears pale, like she used to, pre-Jack.

'How are you doing?' Dawn asks.

Kath shrugs. 'Okay.'

'Has Jack tried to call you?'

Kath shakes her head. 'Anyway, it would only upset me if he did. I'm trying to get back into my dissertation, but it's hard. At this point I'm not sure what I'm going to do.'

'But what about your Ph.D.?'

'I don't know. I think my dissertation's beginning to petrify.'

'Like my life,' says Dawn.

Kath's expression betrays impatience, then slips back into neutral.

'I'm trying to have a better attitude,' Dawn says. 'I'm just not succeeding all that well. There's this married man —'

'Married?' Kath says sharply.

'He's charming, he's persistent, I'm lonely.' Dawn shrugs.

'So you slept with him?'

'No, I didn't. But I'm starting to feel like he's breaking me down.'

Kath's eyes flicker brightly. Her forehead tenses and her lips part; she is on the verge of saying something, but doesn't.

'Go on, say it.' Dawn urges.

'It's your business,' Kath says, 'not mine.'

'You don't approve. You think I'm getting myself into big trouble just thinking about it. You think I'm going to become one of those shrivelled up, overdressed, former mistresses who ride the buses of New York. You think I'm desperate and I'll never meet an available man who really wants me.'

'You're projecting. I don't think that.'

'Then what do you think?'

After a pause, Kath says, 'I think you'll probably get hurt. I think you should be careful. You're not involved with him yet so I think you should steer clear of the whole situation.'

'Yes,' Dawn says unconvincingly, 'you're right.'

Kath smiles. 'You're my best friend, I'll love you and support you no matter what.'

'Me, too,' Dawn says. 'If we were in third grade, we'd be pricking our fingers about now.'

Kath shakes her wet hand, flinging watermelon juice through the air. 'Oh great god of friendship, bond us, we are one!'

'Ooma booma ya ya ya!'

They laugh.

Dawn says, 'I think we should do something, something spontaneous, life enforcing, something a little wild.'

'Like what?'

Dawn thinks for a few moments. 'Dinner and a movie?'

Kath chuckles. 'I'll check the listings.'

'Great. I'll go pee.'

Sitting on the can with her stockings at her ankles and her skirt hiked up on her thighs, Dawn's focus happens to land on a green and black checkered toothbrush dangling next to Kath's red one in the holder above the sink. It is suddenly, unmistakably familiar — for she herself purchased this fancy oral hygiene tool for New Wavers who don't mind spending a little extra to heighten the pleasure of even the day's smallest moments. That was pretty much what she wrote in the little card, attached to the wrapped toothbrush, when she gave it to Hank. Adrenaline rips through her as she hoists up her stockings, flings down her skirt and flushes the toilet. She steps to the sink with resolution and stares at the toothbrushes, side by side, like lovers. But she has to be sure, so she slides the checkered one out of the slot and examines it for evidence, which she instantly finds: two long scratches, one on either side, from Dawn's metal toothbrush holder that was installed when they renovated her apartment. Kath's toothbrush holder is white porcelain, built right into the wall, with nice roomy slots. The facts are clear: Hank has been here — overnight.

Suddenly she is overcome by anguish. She could expect anything from Hank after what's happened. But Kath? If anyone had asked if she would believe that her best friend was capable of deception, the answer would have been a definite *no*. A new, awful truth ruptures into her already dim reality: Kath and Hank. That they have been so good at keeping their secret only makes it worse, a tighter conspiracy, a deeper betrayal.

Dawn replaces the toothbrush and returns to the living room, where Kath is tying her sneakers to go out.

'Ready?' Kath asks.

Dawn says, grimly, 'I'm going home.'

Kath is clearly shocked by the sudden reversal. She studies Dawn's face, which is pale and stony, set in an expression of reticence. 'Why?' she asks, baffled.

Dawn mutters, 'I'll be in touch,' (a lie), collects her things and leaves. She doesn't even say goodbye to Dr. Johnson, which Kath recognizes as a sure sign of deep trouble.

Dawn runs down the stairs and bursts miserably onto sun-drenched Broadway. She rushes into the subway and feels comforted by the cool dank tunnel, as if she now belongs to this descent into darkness. She stands on the edge of the platform, heart pounding, searching compulsively for any flicker of the round red sign of the Number One train. Nothing. A seed of malfeasance has taken hold in her karma, she thinks; and in her desperation, she resolves to try anything, even poison, to root it out.

Nat Weatherhoff, publisher, lives with his wife Helena in a Riverside Drive penthouse with a magnificent view of the Hudson River. The evening sun casts the WeatherhofTs large living room in a soothing peachy amber, a romantic glow. The Weatherhoffs host this annual party in their penthouse for management, and everyone who isn't on vacation is here, many with their spouses or significant others.

Dawn has dressed deliberately in a tight black dress and black patent leather sandals with very high heels. She has had her nails done in a classic red for the occasion, and bought a new lipstick to match. She flits in and out of the conversation clusters of various colleagues, holding a glass of white wine, feeling the warm confidence of alcohol take effect. Gregg's eyes are pinned on her, and she knows it, and each time their gazes cross she feels a surge of heat. Somewhere in this room, she knows, is his wife.

Just as the hors d'oeurves run out and the dinner buffet is being laid by rented maids in black and white uniforms, Dawn revs up her courage and makes her move. She approaches Gregg cheerfully, just as Janice moves away from him and a short pregnant woman with a crisp blond haircut moves toward him.

Dawn delivers a vivacious, professional, 'Hello!' expecting to engage him in a conspiratorial romantic exchange. Instead, he stiffens and says, 'This is my wife, Anna,' and gently touches the shoulder of the pregnant woman.

Dawn casts a gloriously animated smile upon the pregnant woman, and says, 'How nice to meet you.' Her bright gaze falls directly on the huge belly.

Anna smiles wryly, and says, 'Yes, it's real.'

'I thought maybe it was a pinata.' Dawn attempts charming laughter. Anna looks at her husband, bemused.

'This is Dawn Waterston, from editorial,' Gregg tells his wife.

Anna nods. 'Nice to meet you.'

'Gregg didn't mention he was expecting,' Dawn says casually.

'Well, he isn't exactly,' Anna says. 'I am.'

That night, tucked safely in her bed, Dawn dreams that she is in her office with Anna's baby asleep on her lap. Anna comes in with a bag of groceries, rattles something off in Spanish and both women laugh. Dawn turns to the window and sees Gregg in an office across the street, pacing back and forth as he talks on the phone. He is stark naked. Dawn's phone rings. She answers it and hears Gregg talking to a woman. She throws her phone through the window and suddenly her belly puffs up and she is wearing a yellow polka-dotted maternity dress. Anna digs into the grocery bag and hands her a steaming ice cream cone. Chocolate. Her favorite.

The next morning at six-thirty, Dawn's phone rings. She answers in a daze. It's Gregg. Her sleepy mind registers 'tell her' and 'couldn't understand.'

Adrenaline starts to wake Dawn. 'What?' she says. 'What did you say?'

'I said she knows about us. She sensed something. I had to tell her. She doesn't understand.'

'What do you mean "us"?' There is no "us", Gregg. We haven't done anything!' She slams down the phone and it rings again almost immediately. She says, 'That was a stupid thing to do.'

'Hey, I was only kidding!'

Relief floods her — she does feel a little guilty, after all — and she sinks into her pillows. Then anger bubbles up. 'You stupid ass, how could you call me from home? How could you do that to her?'

'I'm not at home, I'm at a pay phone around the corner from you.'

Dawn says, 'I liked Anna, she seems very nice.'

There is a pause. 'Can I come up for a cup of coffee?'

She considers the wide range of possibilities implicit in the request, and mutters, vaguely, 'Coffee? I guess it couldn't hurt.'

And it doesn't, not at all. Condoms and nonoxynol-9 may save Anna and her baby, if responsibility, consideration and good sense do not.

Seventeen
Christine's Revenge

At last, Hank's alloted week of recovery has passed and now he can call Dawn with a clear conscience. One week Chris-free has changed his outlook on life. He can concentrate on work. He eats what he wants, and when, and with whom. He returns to an orderly room at night. He rests, he reads, he remembers his dreams.

Just last night he dreamed of Dawn. He had a crystal clear vision of himself sitting in his office, dialing the phone. He sees each button precisely as he dials her office number.

He means business, and when he calls to resume a love affair, he does so during office hours. He hears the stacatto roll of the phone ringing on her side; the mellow sound of Tony's voice answering; the silent suspense of waiting on hold; and finally, Dawn's voice: 'Hello, Hanky, how are you?' In the dream, they instantly rebond. He buys her a diamond ring at Cartier and they are married in a simple, not too expensive wedding by a leader of the Ethical Culture Society. There is a small reception in a friend's apartment, with long-stemmed white roses and champagne. Everyone is happy, especially the bride and groom. *Dawn and Hank.* What a ring that has to it. Reunited, at last. His inner voice tells him she's out there waiting for him. All he has to do is pick up that telephone and summon happiness back into his life.

Yes, Hank thinks, as he lifts the receiver and dials. He feels a surge of life, of love, of hope.

Tony answers, 'Dawn Waterston's office.'

'Hank Lowe here. How are you?'

'Just fine, Hank, how are you?'

'Great. Dawn available?'

'She's on another line, can she call you back?'

'Yes, please. Thank you.'

'My pleasure,' says Tony, and it sounds like he really means it. It's always a plus to get good vibes from the secretary.

Now that he has placed the call, Hank is wildly impatient to talk to Dawn. His plan is to invite her out to dinner, somewhere really special, and re-pop the question immediately. He is a man of action, after all, bent on victory. Nothing can stop him, not even the Blitsky case daunts him now; nothing, except....

A loud, familiar voice outside his office: 'Hey there!'

Garla's voice responds, 'Hi.'

Something clamps in Hank's chest. For a split second he thinks it's a heart attack. Then he smells the thick perfume: sweet spice. It's Chris. He bolts up and dashes around his desk. Somehow, he must escape. But there's only one way out, through the front door. The only other option is to jump out the window, but then he might miss Dawn's call, and there's the distinct possibility of instant death. A picture of himself sprawled on Park Avenue flashes into his mind, along with a *POST* headline: 'Brilliant Young Attorney Leaps to Death.' He feels a moment of satisfaction. Then, terror.

Christine is standing in his doorway.

'Chris!' he says, trying to sound cheerfully surprised. 'What brings you ... I mean, it's good to see ... Chris, you look *great.*'

Her hair is now coal black, a straight blunt cut with bangs. It looks like a helmet. She's wearing phosphorescent blue mascara and blood red lipstick. Black lace underwear shows through her white linen dress. She says nothing, just stands there intent on torturing him with her stare.

'So, you got my letter?'

'Didn't you get the certified receipt?' she says.

Hysteria pounds in Hank's chest. He doesn't know what to say, do or think, so he buzzes Carla's intercom and asks, 'Carla, did you get the receipt for the letter we sent Chris?'

Carla sighs. 'Yes, Hank, I put it on your desk two days ago.'

'So!' he says to Chris. 'Why don't you sit down?'

She does not move.

'How've you been?' he asks.

'Great.' In her voice is the sound of an oncoming storm. 'You?'

'Me? So so. It's hard, I mean, I'm heartbroken, but, you know . . . .'

She holds up her left hand and the diamond and emerald ring sparkles. 'I thought we were engaged.'

Hank feels awful about all this, really he does. But what can he say? He's just a man, a solitary human being struggling in the Great Conundrum of the late twentieth century, trying to do his best.

'We *were* engaged,' he says, over the sound of the bleeping telephone, 'but as I explained in my letter, my feelings have changed. I'm not ready for marriage. I need to be alone right now, to think things through. The truth is, I can't be with any-one right now, you or anyone else. I'm sorry.'

The phone interrupts. Carla announces: 'Dawn, returning your call.'

'Dawn?' Chris says, *'Dawn?'*

'I can't imagine why she's calling me,' he says. Then, loudly to the intercom, 'I'm in a meeting!'

'Returning your call,' Chris says. She steps forward and Hank's will dissolves.

'I don't know what to say,' he says, and means it. 'It's not that I don't love you, Chris . . . but honey, this is just not for me.'

She's standing in front of his desk now and he's behind it. She smiles. 'Yes it is, Hank. It has to be.'

'Just cancel the wedding, *please*. Don't worry about the money.'

Her eyes sparkle like diamonds glinting in a dark cave. She says, 'I'm pregnant.'

The word boomerangs around his mind, echoing: *pregnant, pregnant, pregnant.* The room fogs around Chris's sharply colorful face. With her helmet of dark hair, she looks like Darth Vader: conqueror, harbinger of doom. She stares at him with a pernicious smile.

Finally, he speaks. 'Pregnant? But Chris, you couldn't be.'

'Ha!' she says, just like that: 'Ha!'

'But what about contraceptives? What about your diaphragm?'

She sighs, as if she's already been through all this in her own mind and the question is redundant. 'I guess I forgot to use it,' she says. 'Anyway, there's a risk factor to birth control. All I know is I'm carrying your child.' She wiggles her ring finger, creating a significant sparkle.

'Are you sure it's mine?' Hanks asks, and instantly receives the quick and painful wrath guaranteed by such a question:

'What? How could you, Hank? Do you think I've been sleeping around? Is that what you really think? After all our time together, after all we've shared, after the way we've loved each other, Hank, how could you treat me like this?' She begins to weep and slumps into the guest chair. 'First you leave me, then you deny your own child.' Her mascara-runny eyes snap to his face, as she says, 'You'll just kick a dog when she's down, won't you!'

Now Hank is seized with the most stupendous guilt he has experienced in all the thirtyish years of his life. It grabs him by the neck and drags him to the floor. He forgets all the bad times, all the lies she has told, all the bitching and demanding and controlling and manipulating. Hank completely forgets everything that led him to the drastic step of leaving her, mid-wedding-arrangements — he even momentarily forgets about Dawn — and becomes a puddle of indiscriminate sympathy.

'Oh, Chrissy,' he says, coming around the desk to join her. She whimpers as he embraces her. 'I'm sorry. Please forgive me. I would never hurt you intentionally. Shh, shh, it's going to be okay.'

Breathing spasmodically, Chris manages to say, 'Then we'll still get married?'

It does not occur to him to research this situation as he would any important case: to request pregnancy verification; wait for a blood sample; discuss termination of pregnancy; or consider a mutually acceptable paternity settlement. Instead, he impulsively takes the quickest route away from her anger, and says: 'Of course we will.' He lays his hand on her belly, which feels as flat as ever, and coos into her ear, 'Our child.'

Chris nods. 'When will you be home?'

'As soon as I can get my things. In time for dinner.' Hank, as he speaks, rapidly becomes depressed. But what can he do? He is a man of honor. How can he just abandon Chris and his child? Besides, if the office ever got wind of this, his career would be finished.

'I'm sick,' she says. 'I can't cook.'

'Of course not. We'll go out.'

'And Hankypoo, just so you know, I hired a maid.'

Hank blinks. More expense. But at least the place will be clean. He says, 'Fine, of course.'

'Well,' she says, 'I'd better get back to work.' She pecks him on the forehead, surveys him briefly and bounces out.

The door swings behind her, clapping shut like his heart. He wonders if their child will resemble her, and sinks into his chair, entranced, benumbed and doomed.

Eighteen

Truth is Stranger than Fiction

Jack sits alone in his lonely apartment in the lonely borough of Brooklyn, reading *SPY*. His basement studio is dark, except for one forty watt bulb by which he reads. Everything is coated with dust. 'Only the dead know Brooklyn,' said Thomas Wolfe in a book Jack read way back in school. If only real life were as easily encapsulated as a story tucked between the covers of a book. If only fiction were stranger than truth, instead of the other way around. If only he could author his own life, instead of letting it author him. If only he had seized the day, then he wouldn't now be reduced to solitude, irregularly peppered with undesirable dates. Jack, man among men, has found himself dating women he doesn't even like. But a man must do what a man must do, and real men, like Jack, being biologically urgent, like Jack, must have sex. That'sjust the way it is.

He puts down the magazine, picks up a yellow legal pad and makes a list of all the women he has slept with in the past year: Janice, Anabel, Susan, Maria, Laurie, Wendy, Kath, Joanna, Ellen, Chris. That's ten different women; he has shared only one-tenth of his annual sexual prowess with his true love, Kath. Could there be something wrong with him? Why can't he just cut through all the fluff and be with the woman he loves? It's true, he is only thirty-one. But still, having found the woman of his dreams, shouldn't he be with her?

Jack doodles around the edges of the list. He doesn't remember why he slept with half of them. Some, he wasn't even attracted to, and others, he just didn't like. And that last one! Sleeping with Chris was fun while it was happening, but afterwards he felt filthy. What he did was wrong, not just because Chris is engaged, or because of his affinity for Hank, but because it was wrong for him. She made him feel dirty and used, like an old condom tossed into the sea. She called him up and somehow — how, who knows? — got him to meet her for a drink. Then she somehow got him to invite her back to his place. By then she had him good and drunk, and she took him right there on the floor before his jeans were at his ankles. Then she stripped him and had him on the bed. Then, later, she got up, dressed and left. That was it. No condom, no diaphragm, no phone call. Nothing. Not that he wants to hear from her, but it just seems so sleazy to have-sex-and-run. There is an etiquette to sex politics, after all, especially in this Age of AIDS. One preserves one's sense of righteous cleanliness. One calls within a few days following the act, if only to deliver a shoddy excuse as to why one can never see you again. Jack always calls. Does Chris think that just because she paid for the drinks, she has the right to sex, gratis?

At least he had the satisfaction of hearing that Hank walked out on her that night. And even though he went back, it proves he's got her number.

One complication of all this is that, days before the event with Chris, Jack signed up on Hank's softball team. The message on Jack's answering machine came as a welcome surprise: 'Hank Lowe here. There's gonna be a softball game, men only, on Sunday the twenty-first. Central Park. Like you to join. Let me know if you can make it. BEEP.' Jack responded in the affirmative. He doesn't know how he'll face Hank now, but the prospect of not going seems too dramatic. So he defaults to his standard solution, and decides to pretend nothing happened.

A good plan, it seems; until after the game, when in a fit of male bonding he finds himself in a bar with Hank and his friend, Andy.

Downtown Beirut is a small, dark dive on lower First Avenue. Jack isn't exactly used to going to fancy places, but really, this is the pits: youths with spiky black hair and pins in their ears, and decrepit alcoholics sitting on ripped black leatherette stools at a long, battered bar. The place is barely lit. Machine guns dangle from the walls.

The three men sit together at the bar and order beers. A waiter with an orange and green checkered afro gives them a bowl of salted peanuts. Conversation takes the normal route: work, sports, women. By the time they're on the latter subject, they have a buzz on and they fly.

'Ann could not get enough of me.'

'Debbie ate me up.'

'Melissa wanted to marry me, but how could I? A girl from Queens?'

'Then there was Roxanne.'

'Take this girl I knew, Sharon, she was . . . .'

Andy's going at it with gusto; apparently, he's a real stud. Jack is impressed. Hank's having a good time, too, and sometimes he throws something in about Chris: the way her nipples tilt slightly upward when excited; the way her hipbones jut out, causing pain (Jack still has the bruises); the way she darts her tongue like a snake. Jack feels like he's dangling on the edge of social catrastrophe. Remembering too well these intimate details about Chris, he fades into a cloud of self-consciousness, fear and guilt.

'So,' Andy says to Hank, 'you're really gonna marry her?'

Hank gulps his beer, swallowing with a grimace. 'Yes.'

'Then you're over that Dawn.'

Jack becomes alert. They couldn't mean Kath's friend, Dawn, could they?

'I took her out, you know,' Andy says, and Hank goes red.

'You went out with Dawn?'

'We had a drink. Period.' Andy's eyes dart to Jack. 'Now I know where I recognize you from. It was that night I went out with Dawn. You were with some girl across the room and Dawn got up to talk to you.'

Ah, yes! Andy was the man across the room, the one Dawn tried *not* to point out.

'I remember,' Jack says.

'You know Dawn?' Hank asks Jack.

'Who was that chick you were out with?' Andy asks. 'Cute.'

'Joanna. Past tense.'

'You know Dawn?' Hank asks again.

'We had a mutual friend,' Jack says. 'Kath.'

Andy says, 'Kath Goodhue? You know her?'

Jack looks at Andy, stunned. Kath would never be interested in a chubby banker type, not with Jack around.

'I know her very well,' Jack says.

Hank is agitated. He pops some peanuts into his mouth and, chewing, asks Jack, 'How well did you know Dawn?'

'Not well, I was going out with Kath. Were you the one Dawn lived with?'

'Yes,' Hank says, sighing heavily, 'that was me.'

'You went out with Kath?' Andy says. 'When? For how long?'

With masculine bravado mixed with unusual sensitivity, a speciality of Jack's, he says, 'I really loved her, but it didn't work out.'

Hank's attention snaps to Andy. 'You didn't go out with Kath, too?'

Andy's pudgy fingers turn white gripping his empty beer bottle. He desperately hails the waiter and orders another round.

Hank's eyes narrow. 'You slept with her, didn't you.'

'With who?' Andy says.

Hank: 'Dawn!'

Jack: 'Kath!'

And like a man caught in the act (better Andy than Jack, anyway), he says, 'Excuse me, I have to go to the bathroom,' and disappears.

Hank and Jack look at each other and smile.

'I think he has a sexual compulsion,' Hank says. 'Except that according to Chris, his real problem is with potency.'

'He slept with Chris, too?'

'Who hasn't?'

Hank laughs. Jack laughs. Hank looks at Jack laughingly, and stops laughing, and says, 'It's really not that funny, is it?'

Jack sobers up fast. 'No, I'm sorry.'

'I don't want to marry Chris,' Hank blurts out. 'I had to say that. Sorry.'

'I understand,'Jack says. 'Kath and I . . . .'

Andy slips onto his stool. He says, 'Kath and I weren't really . . ..' and waves a hand in the air. 'That was just something I said, you know?'

Jack looks at Andy and knows it's a lie, that it's even worse than he thought. No man would deny a liaison that wasn't true. Could they have even been — god forbid — in love? Jack feels sick. Kath with Andy. She deserves much better. Maybe not himself, but someone, anyone, better than this slime.

Andy trickles some peanuts into his mouth and licks his palm with a stumpy tongue. His eyes are glazed: he's drunk. Suddenly, he bolts from the table in the direction of the men's room.

'Hey,' Hank says, 'don't worry about him, he's a jerk. So you and Kath had the real thing, huh?'

'It was special. It would have ended sooner if it wasn't for Dawn. I should have really listened to her. I should have done better than just take her advice, I should have heard what she was saying. I should have been monogo-mous.' He sighs deeply. 'I miss Kath.'

'I miss Dawn,' Hank admits. 'She's got her feet on the ground. Chris . . . .' He shakes his head.

Jack takes a manly swig of beer, swallows with a flex of his Adam's apple and says, 'It's none of my business, but person-ally I don't think Chris can be trusted.'

Hank shakes his head. 'You're right. But there's nothing I can do.'

'Take the bull by the horns,' says Jack. 'It's not too late. Leave again.'

Hank smiles tightly. He blinks. 'She's pregnant. I have to marry her. She's having my baby.'

Unless it's my baby she's going to have, Jack thinks, as the awesome possibility occurs to him. But for all his alleged pride, Jack doesn't have the balls to tell the truth. He could save Hank by hanging himself. But why should he?

He says, 'I guess you're really stuck.'

Hank nods once, definitively. 'Kath mentioned to me there was someone she was in love with. It must have been you. I hope it was. You're a good guy, and that's the truth.'

Jack feels like the little man in the ad, spinning down the toilet bowl. Some friend. Some truth. He'll end up in the sewer if he doesn't pull himself together, and he knows it.

<u>*Nineteen*</u>
Chicken Wings

Kath's hair has grown to three inches and now falls neatly on her head. She combs it back behind her ears with a heavy dose of gel. In her black dress and pale lipstick, she feels almost beautiful. Almost. An intractable loneliness twangs between her ribs, in some unidentifiable empty space. Lately she has found that her contentment in solitude has transmuted into restlessness, and she welcomes even a time-consuming errand like going all the way across town just to pick up a book. Professor Banks wants her to read an essay which is in a rare first edition currently in his son's possession. 'The Peculiar Plight of the Picaro in Eighteenth Century English Society' is probably worth two tokens and a bus ride through Central Park, she reasons. She grabs her leather purse and a colorful shawl and switches off the light.

Dr. Lenny Banks lives in a fourth floor walkup in a tenement used for low-cost hospital housing. The brick-red paint in the hallway and stairwell is peeling, the black linoleum is ripped, the heavy light fixtures are caked with dust. She rings the bell, and after what seems like a long time, she hears footsteps from within. Lenny unlocks the door and a black cat springs between his legs and into the hall.

'Boswell!' He chases the cat down the hall, ambushes her and grips her to his chest.

'I have a Dr. Johnson,' Kath says, following him into the apartment. 'Your dad's influence reaches far and wide, it seems.'

He says, 'Indeed. Would you like some tea? I was just making some.'

She doesn't hesitate, feeling confident that this stranger, her professor's son, is probably not a psychokiller. He is younger than Kath expected, perhaps thirty-three, and far better looking than his father. While Professor Banks is a small, thin man with a wily face and greying blond hair disarranged by a series of cowlicks which make it impossible for him to ever appear neat, Dr. Banks is taller and bulkier, with pale blond hair too thick to reveal a cowlick, sleepy brown eyes and a ruddy, open face. He is handsome, a man who will age well naturally.

'Peppermint, cammomile or orange blossom?'

She answers, 'Peppermint, please.'

He disappears into the kitchen, off a T-shaped hallway which seems to connect quite a few rooms. She moves left and finds herself in a somewhat barren looking bedroom, even messier than her own. Back to the hallway, she turns right and this time finds a cluttered living room which she discovers has a connecting door to the kitchen. He is standing at the counter, dunking tea bags into two mugs of steaming water.

'Hi,' she says. 'I got a little lost.'

'Just don't look in the bedroom,' he says. 'It's been a wreck ever since my wife moved out.' He carries the steaming mugs from the kitchen to the living room, where he sets them down on his coffee table. He sits on the couch and Kath joins him.

'How long has she been gone?' she asks.

Lenny hesitates, then says, 'She left six months ago. Madelaine's a resident in obstetrics, and it got to the point that we pretty much only saw each other at the hospital. She felt swamped by the marriage, she said she wanted her time off to be "free from expectation and disappointment." I guess she just didn't want to be married to me.'

'Are you getting divorced?'

'I'm sure we will,' he says and blows on his tea. 'But me, I'm a person who needs to be married. I've realized that I've got to move on.'

* * *

'Chicken wings?' Dawn says, peering into a large bowl full of pale yellow, shrivelled wings. 'Why didn't he just get regular chicken?'

Kath shrugs.

'What time is he coming back?'

'He said around eight.'

'And the other guests?'

'Eight.'

Dawn laughs. Kath feels ashamed. It was Lenny's idea to have this dinner; it's his apartment, his friends, his menu, and here she is in his kitchen cooking a meal she doesn't even know how to prepare.

'I don't get it,' Dawn says. 'What's with this guy?'

Kath says, 'Let's just cook.' She already feels defeated by this meal. Originally, she was an invited guest; then Lenny called her from the hospital, frantic, saying there was an emergency and asking her to help prepare the dinner for nine people. Just cooking, he said; he had already shopped. Kath was strangely flattered that he felt comfortable enough to ask her. Since they met nearly three weeks ago, they have been out together several times, on sheerly platonic dates; and now they are friends, fast buddies. But after she impulsively agreed to help him, and they arranged for her to get his keys from the super, she remembered that she didn't know much about cooking, and realized that she had never thrown a dinner par-ty. So she in turn begged Dawn's reluctant help, enticing her with the prospect of meeting Lenny's fraternal twin, Randy.

Dawn crushes garlic into hot olive oil and Kath bastes the wings in a lemon/honey mixture. They toss the first few into the pan. The oil sizzles.

Only thirty-four chicken wings to go.

Salad, cold pasta, garlic bread. They set the table for ten.

At seven-thirty the bell rings. Kath answers it nervously. A smiling man with two bottles of wine introduces himself.

'I'm Randy,' he says cheerfully. 'Lenny called me and said you might need help.'

She ushers him in, saying, 'I think we're in pretty good shape, but I'm glad you're here. I'm worried that Lenny won't get here in time for his friends.'

'Knowing him, he won't,' Randy says. He is an attractive man, and Kath is struck by the similarity between the twins. Though they are not identical in either genes or temperament, they share features: large bones, dark eyes, thick wavy hair. Kath can also see that they differ in the tenor of their confidence: Lenny's is high-pitched, on the verge of arrogance, while Randy's is steady and comfortable.

He opens a bottle of wine and pours them all a glass. Dawn, suddenly hostessing with energy, arranges crackers in a shallow basket and hands Randy a wedge of Jarlsberg cheese to unwrap and place on the cutting board. He complies, and follows her to the living room with the rest of the hors d'oeurves arranged on a tray.

Kath finishes up in the kitchen while Dawn and Randy sit in the living room, talking. Then, shortly past eight, the other guests begin to arrive.

Mary and Harry, aged twenty-nine and thirty-four, respectively. She is small and dark and pretty, a furniture designer; he is a portly Irishman covered with red hair and freckles, by day a lawyer, by night a poet.

Lisa and Ted, aged thirty and thirty. She is long of limb, face and hair, a ballerina; he is of blond, rugged good looks, an accountant by day, a football fan by night.

Arianna and Ned, aged thirty-one and thirty-five. She is a hearty, brown-haired, stylishly attired investment banker, who evidently works out; he is a hearty, brown-haired, well-dressed investment banker interested in sailing.

Kath feels acutely uncomfortable. She can't help noticing that, while the women keep looking at her, only the men are actually speaking to her. She answers their questions and waits impatiently for Lenny. It's nearly nine o'clock, all the cheese is gone and there are no more hors d'oeurves. The chicken wings have been warming in the oven for over an hour.

Finally he arrives, wearing his hospital garb of green cotton slacks and V-necked, short-sleeved shirt. He looks exhausted, with dark rings under his eyes and two days' growth on his face. He greets his friends, pets Boswell and kisses Kath on the cheek.

They — his friends — don't like it. He is *her* man, a *husband*. 'Lenny!' his friends singsong. 'So good to see you. How nice of you to invite us. How is Madelaine?'

Lenny manages to steer the conversation in other directions, and Kath is grateful for his deflection of his friends' misplaced, jealous interest in her. The assumption that they are lovers fascinates and disturbs her; fascinates, as evidence that people can't get their minds off sex; and disturbs, with the implication that the platonic nature of their relationship, despite a quality of *dating* to their frequent meetings, is more based on evasion and fear than friendship.

The guests are ushered to the table by an affable Lenny. When Kath presents the wings on a large round serving platter, Mary asks, 'Is this Maddy's old recipe?' and Lenny answers, 'Yes.' There is a cacophony of delight among Lenny's, and Madelaine's, friends.

Afterwards, there are a dozen leftover chicken wings, which Kath puts in a plastic bag and stashes in the fridge. She feels unsure of how to proceed. Lenny put her up to something tonight, and she isn't sure what. Did he know, in advance, that he wouldn't be home in time? But why? Why that recipe? Why those wings?

Dawn hovers in the kitchen, and with her recent cool edge — somewhat warmed by wine and the effects of Randy — tells Kath directly: 'I've seen this before. I've *done* this before. He wants his wife to hear he's got a new woman, to intrigue her, make her jealous, make her remember that he's desirable.'

'But he says it's over.'

'He's still married.'

Kath flashes an accusing look at Dawn, who for a moment appears angry, then laughs. 'Well, I guess I ought to know.'

'I'm glad you came tonight,' Kath says.

Dawn shrugs, and says nothing. 'Randy's nice. What time is it? I almost forgot to make a call.' She lifts the receiver of the kitchen phone and dials a number from memory. After a minute, she hangs up. 'He isn't there. He's usually on time.'

'Do you actually call Gregg at home?'

'Never. We use a pay phone. Did I tell you the news? He's naming his daughter after me! His wife is due in two weeks.'

Kath considers this duplicitous loving of a married man. She doesn't want a pay phone of her own, and in that instant decides that she will never again make Madelaine's chicken wings. She will have to make this clear to Lenny until he is divorced or available, whichever comes first.

After all the other guests have gone, and Randy has Dawn's phone number tucked into his jeans pocket, Kath and Dawn prepare to leave together. They are standing by the door, when suddenly Lenny rushes into the kitchen and returns with the bag of chicken wings. 'Take these,' he says, handing them to Kath. 'I won't be here to eat them.' He kisses her cheek and pats her on the back.

Going down in the elevator, holding her bag o'wings, Dawn looks at Kath with a strangely satisfied expression that seems to say she has somehow deserved this.

Twenty
Victory!

There it is, the book, propped on Dawn's desk for all to see: five-hundred-plus pages of dirt and sleaze, with a resplendent Mike Blitsky standing full self on the cover, smiling at the public from within a tailored, hot-pink suit. He's beautiful, she thinks. Anyway, he's her ticket up. She just knows that *The Memoirs of Misled Mike Mauvais and His Marvelous Men* is going to be a big hit.

In two hours, Gregg is meeting her to take her to the party. It will be just like a regular date, their first. Anna is still in the hospital; it was a complicated birth, but both mother and daughter (little Dawn) are doing well now. Dawn can't wait to see the pictures of her namesake. She has barely had a word with Gregg for almost a week, they spoke only long enough to make this date.

Tony comes in, smiling. 'Here they are,' he says, dropping a heavy box onto her desk with a thud. 'Forty books. Do you think that's enough?'

'Get us another twenty. We're gonna plaster that party with these.'

'No problem.'

'Seven o'clock.'

'See you there.'

Ah, victory! She swivels around in her chair and takes a good look at her colorful, organized office. A good last look. Three years in this room, and now, upward and onward. She can smell her promotion in the air. She can taste it. She can see it: a corner office with two windows, a large desk piled with choice manuscripts — future bestsellers, all — Tony holding court with *his* assistant. Yes, the sweet taste of success is good; she has worked hard for this; made sacrifices for this; and finally, she has arrived. She wheels herself over to the window and looks down at the masses as they throng into the subway. Ha! Let all those bridge-and-tunnel people go back to their boroughs and burbs; leave Manhattan to Dawn.

She grabs her briefcase and two copies of the book (Tony will bring the rest to the party) and goes downstairs to catch a taxi home. No more subways for Dawn, she'll take cabs to and from work from now on. She hails one. It screeches to a stop. 'Uptown,' she instructs. She gets in and slams shut the door. The cab careers to the left and her body sways to the right. Who is she? She is part Ayn Rand, part Judith Krantz, part Cleopatra and part Mrs. Fields.

She is everywoman, anywoman, she has her-own-story now.

Buzz buzz buzz-
'Yes?'
'Get me Chris at her office.'
Hank to Carla. She'll get a little raise with his big promotion. His boss called him in the day after the trial at which, admittedly, Mike Blitsky was acquitted on the grounds that admissible evidence — the movie star, the governor's aide and the senator's wife — was summarily dismissed by the court, and said, 'Hank, you've done a commendable job with this Blitsky case. The board has voted unanimously to offer you a partnership in this firm.' As simple as that.
'Chris on line one.'
'Chris honey, do you want to meet at home or at the River Club?'
'I'm crazed, can't get outta here until the last minute, meet you there.'
'Fine.'

'Oh — and I'd like to bring a friend from work. Okay?'

'Who?'

'You don't know him. He's the new receptionist. I invited him without thinking. Sorry.'

'Don't worry, that's fine.'

Anything would be fine with Hank today. *This is his day.* Chris can do whatever she wants, from exorbitant weddings to unplanned babies, and Hank wouldn't blink an eye.

He waits until quarter to seven — a partner should not leave too early — then dashes home to change into his tuxedo. He arrives to a clean apartment. Hiring that maid was one of the best things Chris has done. Sure, it costs him, but so what? With his promotion, he also got a big raise. He opens a beer and sits on his leather recliner, reeling in the dream of his new reality. Life is good, he thinks ....

And then the phone rings.

'Hank.' It's Dawn. 'I just wanted to congratulate you. I know how hard you've worked. This is your victory, not just Mike's.'

Hank's heart races. He can't deny that he still loves her, but what can he do? Chris is pregnant, they're getting married.

'I got my partnership,' he says.

'Great! I'm really happy for you, Hanky.'

Why does she sound so happy about it? After all, if things had worked out between them, she'd be married to a partner. Doesn't she care?

'You sound good, Dawny. How's the book?'

'Fabulous! I'll give you a copy tonight. I just wanted to have a word with you privately, without all those people around, you know? Can you believe it, Hank? We've made it.'

'We sure have.'

After the call, Hank's mood plunges. What kind of a victory is this, to live without his true love? Who are his real friends? Is he becoming one of those men whose personal life is disingenuous and whose social life consists of business acquaintanceships? Jack Green, he thinks; Jack could be a real friend.

* * *

Jack has never been to the River Club, but he's seen it in passing along the FDR Drive. They're always having fancy parties and weddings there. Once, he saw Trump's former sleek white yacht, *The Princess,* docked outside. He takes a lint brush and beats his tuxedo, a costume from one of the road shows he travelled with in the old days, and removes the profuse orange fur of his cat Chop Suey. Now all he needs is a date. With a pumping heart, he dials Kath. Maybe she's free tonight. Maybe she still loves him. Maybe .... 'Hi, this is Kath, I can't come to the phone right now, so please leave a message, and I promise I'll call you back. BEEP.' But he doesn't trust a machine's promise to return a call. He hangs up.

Kath hurries into her apartment to change for the party. She hears her phone machine beep, and a click. She hates it when people hang up on her machine; she needs every call she can get. And lately, she's been hoping Jack would call again. She could always call him, but she feels too confused; she doesn't know what, or who, she really wants; and there's Lenny. He'll be by momentarily to pick her up. She turns on the radio, eats a cold chicken wing and cuddles with Dr. Johnson for a few minutes before deciding what to wear.

Dawn can feel the electricity in her hand, which rests on the phone receiver. She can feel her power. Calling Hank like that — without hesitation, without fear, with sheer confidence — was a coup. Maybe she's getting over him, after all. Let Chris have him! she thinks, with uncharacteristic cavalier abandon. She revels in this rare sensation that life can be good ....

Then the phone rings.

'Hi, babe,' says Gregg.

'Are you running late?'

'I'm not running at all.' He sighs. 'I can't come. They're letting Anna and Melissa out of the hospital tonight, I just found out.'

'Melissa? I thought you named her Dawn.'

He laughs. 'Why would we do that?'

Dawn slams down the receiver. She unplugs the phone and paces angrily. And finally, at long last, she screams.

The sun is setting in the west like a big red ball descending into the Hudson, and an orange glow reflects off the shimmery East River. The River Club glitters with strings of little white lights laced into trees that stand like guards outside, outlining the door and plate glass windows. Waiters in white tuxedos bustle on the outdoor balcony. Twilit silhouettes move like shadows inside.

Randy happily escorts Dawn in. She glows, albeit with suppressed anger, in her spangled peach dress (purchased for her engagement party, never worn). This is her night, and she won't let Gregg — or any man — ruin it.

Mike Blitsky, wearing a gold lame caftan and silver slippers, has formed a receiving line of himself and seven highly decorative Men. The party is stocked with the notorious consorts, exotic lure to all the other guests: journalists, lawyers, employees of Dick, Lesser & Moore and of Weatherhoff.

'Darling!' Mike extends a deliberately limp hand. He is the first on the receiving line, which snakes from the front door and up four steps, with Marvelous Men like candles on a tiered cake. 'You look fabulous!'

'So do you,' Dawn says, leaning toward him. He stamps her cheek with a silver kiss. 'Congratulations, Mike.'

'I deserve it. And so do you. And so does Hank. Goddess, but I must admit, I am deeply relieved!'

'But you never seemed very worried.'

'I hid it. Remember, I'm a professional.'

Dawn laughs. 'This is Randy Banks,' she says.

Randy looks at Mike with a deadpan expression and nods soberly. Dawn is aware of the strange first impression Mike makes, and how it is contradicted by his warmth when you come to know him. It momentarily pains her to see Randy's cold reaction; then she remembers that Mike is used to this. He ignores it, and says, 'Romeo's already here, sweetheart. He came alone.'

Dawn goes weak with sadness. If Hank was coming alone, why didn't he ask her to join him? she thinks; and immediately recognizes the absurdity of that thought.

'Meet my Men,' says Mike, gesturing towards his lineup.

Dawn and Randy go from Man to Man, shaking hands, introducing themselves. There's John, a six-foot five-incher with long red hair, a strapless black top and white leather miniskirt; Larry, plump with a black curly mop of hair and a bright red heart lipsticked over his mouth; Robert, a blond muscleman wearing a leopard-print sarong and lace-up Caesar sandals; Alan, who looks like a macho lumberjack in jeans, work books and a plaid shirt; and . . . Dawn is just meeting Aaron, a short Man in a blue silk dress, when the front door swings open and who should enter but Chris — with Marco.

Dawn stops dead in her tracks and watches, along with Randy and all the Men, who react with curiosity to her reaction of shock. Chris, in a purple leather minidress and wiry helmet of coal-black hair, and Marco, in a grey business suit, are greeted by Mike Blitsky.

Dawn is overcome by sudden nausea, a wave of mixed emotions and various confusions: intense hatred of Chris; resentment that she's here (Hank isn't alone tonight, after all); shock at seeing Marco; confusion at his being with *her*; and hypercuriosity as to how the half-brothers will greet each other. She wonders if she is the only one who knows of that connection, and looks from face to face. *Nothing*, no reaction, zip. Could she have been wrong about Mike and Marco? Blitsky acts as if he has never seen the man before. And macho Marco is aloof; he responds to Blitsky as if he is just another guy, not the kind of flaming freak Dawn knows Marco hates, certainly not his brother. Mike smiles, bats his eyelashes, introduces himself, gives Marco and Chris meltingly pudgy handshakes and shoos them along the receiving line.

Randy asks, 'Do you know them?'

'No,' she says, and they go inside.

Dawn has arranged for a display table for the books, and nervously takes copies from a box on the floor and stacks them in a pyramid, which promptly tumbles down. She stacks them again, carefully, with shaking hands.

'Can I help?' Randy offers.

'No thanks, I can do it myself.'

Once again, the books come crashing down.

'Relax,' Randy orders, laying a warm hand on her shoulder and squeezing the knotted muscle. 'Let me do it.' He calmly arranges the books into an even pyramid and steps back. 'There,' he says, 'that looks solid.'

Dawn says, 'Where's the bar?'

Randy fetches her a glass of wine and a beer for himself, and they go in search of familiar faces. The party is already lively. She sees Jack across the room, looking dapper in a tuxedo, laughing with a Man in a shimmering black spandex bodysuit and a young couple. The dark haired man looks familiar, though his heavy-set date, in a shimmering turquoise dress, does not. Then a series of images suddenly emerge: jogging along a sunny surburban street in a badly stained sweatsuit, romance in a laundry room, a too-white smile, the black and chrome apartment where she met Marco. She remembers: David Siedelman, Jack's friend.

'Come,' Dawn says to Randy, 'meet some friends of mine.'

Jack winks when he sees her, and that tiny blink-of-an-eye undams a river of warmth in Dawn.

'Pretty,' he says, and kisses her cheek.

She says, 'Randy, Jack. Jack, Randy.'

They shake.

David cracks a huge, bleached smile. Smooth and polished, he's a real telemodel, a silver-skinned celluloid dummy with quick-flashing images — takes of himself — flickering behind blue-tinted contact lenses. He's an actor, and just as Dawn reels into her automatic skepticism about actors, his companion says:

'Margo Zimmerman. I'm Garth's agent, I was hoping to meet you, we just executed contracts for the *Mauvais* TV movie. Production starts next month, with Garth in the lead.'

'Who's Garth?' Dawn asks.

Margo indicates David.

'Are you playing Mike?' Dawn asks.

David glows a *yes.*

'He's gonna do great,' Margo says, gripping him to her side with linked elbows. Their eyes lock together in a reverie of love/career/party thrills/fame/the fee which will go toward their co-op, not to mention her commission for cutting the deal and three glasses of champagne each, surging through them. They're in love, for real.

'How exciting,' Dawn says.

She notes a quick flare of Jack's nostrils, a subtle roll of his eyes. She knows it, he knows it: these two flakes are L.A. bound.

'Here's my card,' Margo says, plucking a lavendar business card from her patent leather handbag.

Dawn reciprocates with a staid white Weatherhoff card.'The extension may change soon,' she says.

'We'll do lunch,' Margo says, 'one of these days.'

'Definitely,' Dawn agrees. Then, to Randy. 'Shall we?'

She doesn't tell him *what,* yet he agrees instantly, and they go off together. Within a few moments she spots Tony standing by a wall of windows behind which the inky river gleams with reflected light. He's talking to an appealing looking young man, who must be his spouse-equivalent. They're wearing matching red suspenders.

'Dawn!' he says when he sees her. 'I have the books, I got some extras from Publicity.'

She introduces Randy to Tony, who introduces his friend: 'This is Rex, my lover.'

Rex smiles, and says, 'Hi, it's really nice to meet you,' with a distinct Midwestern twang.

Tony's face droops into a pouty frown. His eyes cloud. 'Honey,' he says to Dawn, 'what's wrong?'

'Nothing!'

He nods, clearly skeptical.

'Give me some books,' Dawn instructs. 'You take some, too, and circulate.'

Tony obeys and, with Rex, blends into the crowd laden with books.

Randy carries books for Dawn, staying fast at her heels. She moves through the party in her shimmery dress, with her blonde curls bouncing at her shoulders, smiling, waving, stopping occasionally to bestow a book on anyone she deems important. She is poised and professional, a cardboard silhouette of her real self raging beneath the smooth exterior. Meanwhile she searches, secretly, for Hank.

'Boo!'

Dawn stops suddenly, and there is Kath in a black twenties dress with a frayed hem and seams that pull at her armpits. She looks pale and tired, Dawn notices, and feels a surge of emotion. She misses their former closeness, which she has stridently denied the few times they have seen each other since she spotted Hank's toothbrush. Even now, when she pictures it hanging in the porcelain slot, she automatically recoils.

'Just get here?' Dawn asks coolly.

Lenny answers for her: 'A few minutes ago. I was immediately struck by the flagrant degeneracy of the crowd. Hi, Randy, how goes it? Nice suit.'

'I think it's yours,' Randy says. Lenny winks. Randy shrugs.

'Can I have a copy of the book?' Kath asks. 'I saw the display. There's a hole at the bottom of the pyramid. How did you get it to stand like that?'

Dawn and Randy look at each other, perplexed.

'I'll get Mike to sign it,' Dawn says, handing Kath a book from Randy's pile. 'Have you met him yet?'

'No. Introduce me?'

Dawn scans the room for Mike and spots Hank, heading for the bar. She is seized with anxiety. Chris and Marco follow closely behind.

Kath says, 'But isn't that —'

'Hello!' It's Mike, appearing in their cluster like a flash of gold and silver light. He is carrying a copy of his book.

When introduced to Kath, Mike's eyes open dramatically. He licks the tip of a manicured finger and rifles through the opening pages of the book. ' "Thanks to Katherine Goodhue",' he reads from the acknowledgement page, ' "whose research was invaluable to the completion of this book." So, how did you like Bayonne?' He smiles hugely and hands her the book, still open at the acknowledgements. 'Please sign here.'

Kath signs her name next to where it's printed, as in a yearbook.

'You, too,' Mike instructs Dawn.

She signs next to 'Thanks especially to Dawn Waterston, my editor, who made this the best book it could possibly be.' Her heart takes a leap as it has each time she has read the next acknowledgement: 'And I must also extend my deep gratitude to Henry Lowe, Jr., who during the writing of this book made me a free man.' Mike has not yet garnered Hank's signature.

Mike looks at Lenny and blinks his eyes. 'You look awfully familiar,' he says. 'Do I know you?'

Lenny turns red, and looks at Randy, who returns the baffled expression. The twins shake their heads.

'Pardon me,' says Mike, 'but are you lovers? Leave it to me to flirt with a married man.'

'No!' Randy and Lenny say at once.

Kath says, 'They're twins.'

'Ah! I've always wondered about *in utero* copulation. You know, the genitalia of newborn males are extremely large. Hello!'

It's Hank, Chris and Marco, with Jack trailing. Meaningful glances flash amongst this dense cluster of friends and ex's, sexual tension sizzling like an electric storm. Blitsky is in heaven. He hugs the book to his rotund, gold-clad belly, and watches.

The first thing to strike Dawn is that Hank appears miserable. Her heart lifts. Could there be hope? Chris doesn't look pregnant in that tight purple minidress. And since when do New Age women drink alcohol during pregnancy? That oily amber liquid could only be whiskey. If she isn't careful, Chris is going to give birth to a mongoloid, bug-eyed addict, a mangled mini-Lowe. She weaves her arm through Hank's, and Dawn gets the eyes-off message loud and clear.

Hank greets everyone individually with a small, professional nod: 'Hello, hi, how are you, good to see you.' Dawn knows him well enough to note the special interest he takes in Randy. Is that a flicker of jealousy in Hank's bloodshot eyes? Chris's fuchsia lips tauten and she tugs on his arm.

'This is Chris Lustgarden,' he says.

And Chris adds, 'His fiancee.'

Marco, who stands at Chris's side, looks uncomfortable. His eyes keep flitting to Dawn. Then — she can't help it, she's feeling tipsy and angry and cavalier — she says, 'Hi, Marco, how are you?'

Everyone looks at her.

Kath grins. 'Nice to see you, Marco,' she says.

'Hi, guy,' says Jack.

Jack and Kath look at each other. Then Jack's eyes shift to Lenny, and look away.

A tall black Man in a yellow chiffon gown floats to Mike's side with comfortable familiarity. Mike says, 'This is Roger, my main Man.'

'I need a refill,' Chris says, swirling the ice around her empty glass.

'I'll get you one,' Marco immediately offers.

'I'll tag along.' Chris trots off after him.

Hank looks at Dawn and says, 'He's a temp in her office. How do you know him?'

And she answers, point-blank, 'We had a brief affair.'

Hank's expression freezes, as he absorbs this information. His former fiancee, with a temp? Then he smiles stiffly. She revels in the effect of her statement: that this is not the Dawn he once knew, loved and fled from. No, this is a different Dawn, a bold adventuress, a woman warrior, a senior editor, a sexy blonde. *We had a brief affair.* Ha! Blitsky says, 'And I thought I was the femme fatale.' Roger's laughter bubbles up like champagne, momentarily drawing the group out of its tension with sudden liberating intoxication.

Twenty-One
Four Bottles of Wine and an Unexpected Leap

Dawn looks older. There is something humorless and un-moving around her eyes: deeper crows feet, a heavier gaze, a sense that nothing would surprise her. Even in the dim light of this crowded Indian restaurant, Jack can see Dawn's sadness.

'Maddy's late,' Randy says. 'She's usually so punctual. Something must have happened at the hospital.'

Dr. Madelaine Banks is Jack's blind date. He was sitting on his couch with Chop Suey kneading his thigh, watching football on TV, when the phone rang. It was Dawn, inviting him out to dinner. She didn't mention that his date would be Kath's boyfriend's wife.

A slim Indian waiter, in a burgundy shirt with a Nehru collar, speaks to them in broken English.

'I think he wants us to order,' Dawn says. 'Let's just get some appetizers for now.'

Jack chooses raita. Dawn orders vegetable samosas. Randy gets shrimp poori. They ask the waiter to please open one of the two bottles of wine they have brought. As with most of the Indian restaurants downtown, this one has no liquor license, and if you want to drink it is strictly bring-your-own.

A few minutes later, just as the appetizers arrive, Madelaine Banks hurries in. She is a small, handsome woman with short brown hair and big brown eyes, wearing sneakers, a billowly plaid skirt and a red sleeveless cotton sweater. She strikes Jack as vibrant, rushed, smart and friendly.

'Hi,' she says. 'Sorry I'm late.' She kisses Randy on the cheek and sits down. 'Guess I better catch up.' As she consults the menu, Jack notices the bright gold wedding band on her ring finger. He's no wiseguy, but he's a man, and a man knows when a woman is available. Madelaine is not. It's the ring, the sneakers and her general casualness that tell him she did not come here for the date but for the company and the food. Jack is relieved; he is not game for romance, either.

Madelaine notices Jack staring at her ring. 'My husband and I are separated,' she says, and smiles.

'I know,' Jack says.

Madelaine looks at Randy, at first surprised, but then she shrugs it off. 'Oh well, so what?' she says. 'It's no secret.' She folds her menu. 'I'll have the Tandoori Chicken.'

By the time dinner is fully underway, the small round table is crowded with wine glasses, water glasses, curries, tandooris, poories, broths and chutnies. Randy has disappeared to the liquor store to replenish the supply of wine. They are sated, drunk and happy and have every intention of getting drunker and happier. After all, what more can the modern adult hope for, when you can't do drugs, smoke or have sex; be an addict or help an addict; use paper napkins or plastic wrap gratuitously; or even call a dead man dead — now, he is 'otherwise abled,' an ambiguous handicap to be sure. Sulfites aside, wine on Saturday night for the non-addicted career-stressed sensually-deprived single adult certainly should not be too much to ask of life.

'I can't believe it's Labor Day weekend,' Dawn says. 'I should have gone somewhere for the long weekend. I really need a break.'

'But it's the worst weekend of the year for traffic,' Madelaine says. 'Public beaches aren't safe anymore. Airports are congested. Face it, there's nowhere to go.'

'I'll say I went to Little India,' Jack says, and laughs, though no one else does.

'Anyway,' says Madelaine, 'I'm beginning to think that dreams and wishes and fantasies are only mental tricks to get us through time, to get us to the other end of life. Through Labor Day weekend. Going away doesn't really matter, it's the wish to go away that does. As long as we don't expect our dreams to actually come true, it doesn't matter where we spend the weekend.'

'Cynic,' says Randy. He sits down breathlessly with a paper bag clanking with bottles. 'It's hot out there.'

'I know what you mean,' Dawn says. 'The good things that happened this summer were not what I planned. The good things I planned went *pfft.*'

'Exactly,' says Madelaine.

'I dunno,' says Jack, 'I didn't plan anything.'

They all look at him in silence, registering the obvious fact that he didn't plan anything and nothing happened.

'I planned on swimming twice a week at the gym,' Randy says, 'and I swam twice a week at the gym. And I met Dawn. I'm happy.'

Madelaine smiles lovingly at Randy. 'Did you know that Lenny never wanted to be a doctor?'

Randy looks surprised. 'Sure he did, always.'

Madelaine shakes her head. 'Nope, not really. He had a secret dream, he wanted to be a writer.'

'No!' says Randy.

'Really?' Dawn says. 'Why didn't he?'

Madelaine shrugs. 'Respectability, I guess. I wanted to be a ballerina. Isn't that stupid?'

Jack shakes his head. 'I don't think so,' he says.

'I wanted to be a writer, too,' Dawn says. 'Me and every other editor in New York.'

'I always wanted to be a math teacher,' Randy says. They all laugh: he u a math teacher. 'No, really, I did.'

Jack says, 'I grew up thinking I'd become a doctor.'

'You're joking,' Dawn says. 'Does Kath know that?'

'No, no one, just you guys. Dokta Green. My dad's a doctor. They're not too happy with how I turned out.'

'Oh, forget it,' Madelaine says. 'You can't please everyone. My God, it's hard enough trying to please yourself. Lenny loves the ballet, too, but I don't think he goes much anymore. When we met, we went to the ballet all the time. He told me that if he'd had his way he'd have been a dance critic, he wanted to write about dance. For Lenny, that was the thing.'

'I don't know much about dance,' Jack says. 'We build a lot of sets for City Ballet, though. Just finished *Romeo and Juliet.*'

'That's my favorite ballet! Lenny and I decided to get married after seeing it together.'

Suddenly, out of nowhere, Jack has an idea. He is smitten with an inspiration, a divine gesture of generosity towards another person, a desire to go out of his way just for the hell of it. He says, 'It's Saturday night and no one's at the shop. Let's all go out there and I'll show you!'

The streets of Greenpoint are empty, and once their taxi whizzes away, it is totally silent. Jack unlocks the heavy front door, which creaks with sharp spasms as he opens it, echoing through the huge warehouse space. Dawn says, 'This is creepy.'

'Yodelodelodel!' Randy calls out. The sound hits the ceiling and boomerangs back at them like the singing of some lonely ghost that can't hold a tune. It goes on and on. Randy laughs.

'Shh,' Jack says. And that echoes, too. 'You never know, Katz could be here.' He turns on the overhead fluorescent light, illuminating a maze of colorful sets.

'It's beautiful,' Madelaine says. 'This place is terrific.' 'Come on,' Jack says. 'I'll show you the set.' He leads them through a tiny door in a set for *Alice in Wonderland* and they emerge into a space surrounded by three walls painted with file cabinets from top to bottom. From there, they pass through a suburban backyard with a painted-in swimming pool and lounge chairs;

an arctic winter with penguins; an African jungle with palms, coconuts and monkeys; a nineteenth century living room at Christmas time. They stop in a huge stone dining room with a backdrop depicting an enormous table piled with meat, bread, wine goblets, bowls of fruit and hunks of cheese, surrounded by ornate wooden chairs upholstered in red velvet. A painting of a king hangs on the wall. A mangy cat huddles in a corner.

'This is it,'Jack says. 'Come on, I'll show you the set for the big love scene.'

They walk around the back of the dining room set, and there it is, a huge garden scene for Romeo's moonlit wooing of Juliet: an immense navy, pink and aqua sky, a full pearly moon, a mass of roses and weeds, and a trellis that leads up to a balcony.

'We just finished it,'Jack says.

'This is it!' Madelaine sparks up. 'This is where it happened for Lenny and me. This is where I looked at him and we knew we were going to be married.' She smiles mischievously. 'Can I go up there? Is it safe?'

'Sure.'

'I danced Juliet as a kid. I think I remember some of it.' Madelaine takes a little leap.

Dawn claps.

'Any music?' Randy asks.

'Sure, Mel has some tapes. I'll go put something on.'

'Try to find something classical,' Dawn calls after him.

'Sure, sure, sure,' Jack says, his voice trailing off as the echoes increase.

He goes back through the sets, to Mel's office, up front. It's a small, boxy room full of cabinets and a battered metal desk, crammed with fifteen years worth of files, books and papers. Mel's not exactly what you would call organized. Jack opens the desk drawer and picks through his collection of tapes, looking for something for Madelaine to dance to; but the fact is, he wouldn't know the right piece if it jumped out of the drawer and hit him in the face. So he does what any man would do and wings it, selecting a tape with a painting of a storm on the front. He slips it into the stereo and turns the receiver on.

Wagner's *Tristan and Isolde* blasts. It sounds okay to Jack.

He tosses the plastic case onto the desk and is about to close the drawer when he notices a small photograph stuck in the back. With no attempt to resist his curiosity, he digs through the mess and pulls out the photo. It's an old black-and-white with scalloped edges. A date stamped at the bottom reads May 3, 1965. Standing in the middle of a yard, in front of a white house, is a young Mel. He has brown hair and is thin. In fact, he looks just a few years older than Jack. He looks like a different man, except for his smile, which is the very same gleaming row of silver slabs as now. Jack can hardly believe it: Mel, young and surrounded by kids. The three boys with him seem to range in age from about five to twelve. They're all short and dark and round. Could these be his sons? They look so familiar, just like Mel. Jack is transfixed by the photograph. Mel, long ago, in another life. And there's something about those boys, Jack doesn't know what, but he thinks it'll come to him if he has a visual reference. He slips the photo into his jeans pocket, closes the drawer and shuts off the light.

Dawn and Randy stand near the set, watching Made-laine practice her ballet to the dramatic dronings of Wagner. Jack's no critic, but her pirouettes look a little dizzy to him and her leaps like sheer clutz. Maybe she made the right choice by go-ing into medicine. Anyway, she's having fun tonight, and so are they all. They cheer and applaud as she leaps and spins. As the music crescendos, she dashes behind the set and a few moments later appears on the balcony.

'Awright Juliet!' Randy calls.

'Go for it!' Jack cheers.

Dawn claps. 'You look beautiful!'

In a spasm of excitement, Madelaine gestures to her audi-ence, leaning against the balcony and opening both arms out.

First they hear a loud crack, the sound of splitting wood. Then they see movement in the set: the balcony coming loose at the joints. Then the whole balcony comes hurtling down, tossing Madelaine against the backdrop with a chilling scream and a thud.

Dawn's on her feet immediately, rushing over to her. Randy and Jack follow. They crouch over Madelaine, who is limp against the painted-on brambles and roses.

'Oh my God!' Dawn cries, feeling Madelaine's forehead as if she'd just come down with a flu, not a balcony.

'She has a pulse,' Randy says. 'Don't move her. Call an ambulance. Call Lenny.'

Randy has absolute faith in the healing powers of his older (by three minutes) brother. *Call Lenny* has been the closing refrain of every tragedy of his life. He can't help it, he's a twin. He recites Lenny's number and Jack rushes to the office to make the call.

Dawn, Randy and Jack hover in terror over Madelaine until they hear echoes of a knocking on the front door. Jack springs up and dashes through the sets. He pulls open the door, and there is Lenny — and Kath. Lenny's medical bag dangles from his hand.

'Where is she?' he demands.

'In the back. Follow me.' Jack leads them through the sets to *Romeo and Juliet.*

Lenny rushes to Madelaine and gently adjusts her position. 'She'll be all right,' he finally says. 'She has a broken leg. Call an ambulance.'

'We did,' Randy says. 'Twenty minutes ago.'

'Well where the hell is it?' Lenny turns bright red. 'Damn EMS!'

Madelaine's eyes pop open, and she says, 'Lenny.'

'It's okay,' he says softly.

'I was doing *Romeo . . .*' she mumbles. He finishes her fading sentence: ' *. . . and Juliet.*'

The ambulance arrives. Dawn, Randy, Jack and Kath stand aside as Lenny instructs the medics as to Madelaine's care. They get her onto a stretcher and take her away. Lenny jumps into the back of the ambulance and disappears with Madelaine in a cacophony of sirens and flashing red lights.

'So,' Dawn says, 'can we catch a cab into the city?'

'We have to call a car service,' Jack answers.

They walk slowly through the shop, toward the office and phone. Jack and Kath hang back a few feet.

'That's too bad,' Jack says.

Kath says, 'Poor Madelaine'. She looks very pale, very beautiful, he thinks. 'I'm tired,' she says, and yawns.

'Well . . . you can always stay at my place tonight. I mean, if you don't want to go all the way into Manhattan.'

Kath smiles. And he knows, in that smile, that there's hope. He tells himself: Jack, here she is, go for it.

Twenty-Two

A Little More Peculiar Politics

'Umm, good,' Jack says, sitting naked on Kath's bed, finishing the last chicken wing. He wiggles greasy fingers and she tosses him a tissue. 'I hope you make those again soon.'

Her body slides against him under the covers. She runs her hand slowly over his muscled chest. He tosses the greasy tissue to the floor, moves around to hold her and their bodies loosely weave. And then the phone rings, and they freeze. Dr. Johnson, feline voyeur who sits sphinx-like at the foot of the bed, jumps down and trots over to the phone. They all listen to the message: 'It's Dawn. Well, I'm sitting here looking at an invitation to Hank's wedding. I wonder if he invited all his old girlfriends. What are *you* wearing to the big event?'

Kath wilts in Jack's arms, and he says, 'What was that all about?'

'I don't know what's bothering her,' she says, 'but I'm sick of it. I'm calling her. I'm going to find out.'

Dawn mopes in and plops down on the couch, a safe distance from Kath. Dr. Johnson, displaced, springs to the floor. The sounds of Jack's muted singing and the cascading shower can be clearly heard.

'He messengered an invitation to my office yesterday. I don't understand him. I don't understand any of this.'

'Talk to me,' Kath says. 'Let's *talk.*'

Anger flashes in Dawn's eyes. She hesitates, and finally says, 'He was here.'

Kath nods. 'He needed someone to talk to.'

'Why didn't you tell me? Don't answer — it's obvious.'

'Oh? Then you tell me.'

Dawn is stubbornly silent.

Kath says, 'He asked me not to say anything, so I didn't. He was very confused.'

'Obviously.'

'He sat here and talked. He said a lot about you, how much he still loved you, how ridiculous he felt about everything he did. He didn't talk about Chris. I think he was embarrassed.'

As Kath talks and Dawn listens with an expression resembling confusion, Jack emerges, wrapped at the waist in a red towel. His curly hair glistens wet. He responds to the somber atmosphere by looking from woman to woman, muttering, 'sorry, sorry,' and turning toward the bedroom.

'No, stay,' Dawn says tensely. 'It might be good to have a male point of view.'

Jack considers this for a moment, then shrugs his bare shoulders and sits at the table.

'You know,' Kath says, 'I don't think Hank really has any friends. I think that's why he came to me.'

'I like Hank,' Jack says.

'He deserves better than Chris,' Kath says.

'Who exactly?' Dawn's face is hard, set in a mask of pained resentment. 'I saw his toothbrush in your bathroom. I know he slept here.'

'He spent two nights here, on the couch.'

Dawn stares at Kath stubbornly, hesitant to let go of the anger. Kath nods, understanding at last. She moves closer to Dawn on the couch. 'All this time, you thought we had an affair? You idiot, Hank's in love with you!'

'Definitely,' Jack says.

Dawn bursts into tears. 'Then why is he marrying Chris?'

Kath wraps Dawn in a hug. 'It's terrible,' Kath says, 'but she's pregnant, and you know Hank, Mr. Responsibility.'

'He's a coward. I hate him! Why didn't he make her get an abortion?'

'How could he do that? It's her body, her choice.'

'What about his choice?'

'It seems like Hank doesn't know how to make a choice. Anyway, don't forget that it's his baby, too. Maybe he wants it. Either way, wouldn't it be a Hank-thing to say: I made her pregnant, I have to take the consequences and marry her. In a way, I think he's doing the right thing. If you were a man and you impregnated a woman, wouldn't you feel obliged to take responsibility for the situation?'

Jack tosses a penny into the air, and catches it. He slaps it onto the back of his other hand. 'Heads,' he says. 'The truth.'

They look at him.

'What are you talking about?' Kath asks.

Jack sits at the table, frozen. He seems to want to say something. He seems terrified.

'Nothing,' he says. 'Never mind.'

'Tell us,' Kath says.

'It doesn't matter. I had a thought. It was stupid.'

'Maybe I'll get them something really awful,' Dawn says, 'like a Dustbuster.'

Twenty-Three
Wedding Day Blues

The doorbell echoes into Hank's dream like the gong of doom. Waking, he squints to see the bedside clock's phosphorescent face which reads 7:06 a.m. Who would ring the doorbell this early on their wedding day?

Careful not to wake Chris, he slides into his leather slippers and plaid bathrobe and goes to answer the door. No one is there. Someone, though, has slid an envelope under the door. He picks up the plain white envelope, addressed to him, and opens it. Inside is a letter, typed on plain paper, and when he unfolds it a photograph flutters out. He picks it up from the floor and looks carefully at the old black-and-white photo, with scalloped edges, of a man and three fat boys. Then he reads the letter.

Dear Hank,

I slept with Chris Lustgarden. It was in July. No contraception was used. I am disease-free (don't worry) but I am extremely potent. I can't help it, that's just the way I am. I think you should know this before doing anything drastic. I know you're getting married today so I thought I better tell you this before it's too late.

I also think she is probably having an affair with someone in her office.

BEWARE. This is *your* life.

Anon. P.S. What do you make of this photo?

Hank is baffled. Who could have written such a letter? A friend — does he have any? — or a lunatic? He doesn't have any enemies that he knows of; but then, if you're a lawyer, you never know. He looks at the photo again. The man's teeth seem to sparkle in the sunlight, as if they were some kind of metal. And one of those boys looks awfully familiar. He stares and stares at the boy, trying to get at it. Who is this? Then it hits him: IT'S MIKE BLITSKY. A childhood snapshot of his infamous client. Adrenaline races through him as the realization crystalizes. The other boys must be his brothers, and the man is his father, whose teeth were knocked out by his first wife. He thinks, impulsively: if only Dawn could have incorporated this picture into the book!

But it's too late now. Too late, in many ways. *Dawn.* He's marrying Chris today. Or is he? What about this letter? And what does this photo have to do with the accusations in the letter? It says 'I slept with Chris' and the photo shows Mike Blitsky as a child.

Hank plunges into despair. If the letter is accurate, then he really is doomed. The wedding ceremony is scheduled for four o'clock this afternoon. That gives him nine hours to reach his final decision: *to marry her, or not?* But everyone is coming to the wedding: his colleagues from Dick, Lesser & Moore, his preferred clients, his family, his friends. And now this. Even if the letter is true, how can he back out? He has a reputation to preserve.

He rereads the letter, analyzes it, and weighs the options. What are the messages here? He sits at the kitchen table with a legal pad and a pen, and writes:

1) Chris is unfaithful.
2) The baby may not be mine.
3) I may not be under any obligation to marry her.
4) If so, better get out of it now . . . HOW?
5) Before anything, find out the truth . . . HOW?

What should he do: ignore the letter and go through with the wedding as planned; confront Chris; or not confront her and skip out on the wedding?

Doomed.

He hears footsteps. Chris is awake. He tears the paper off the pad, folds it and puts it in the pocket of his robe with the letter and photo.

Do it, Hank: confront her. This is your life, just like the letter says. He gets up, tightens the sash of his bathrobe, takes a deep breath . . . and waits.

She's in the bathroom — she always goes straight to the bathroom in the morning. Don't just stand there and wait for her, he tells himself, go in there, *seize the day.* He marches to the bathroom and pushes open the door.

'Hey!' she shouts. 'Don't you know how to knock?'

Her coal black hair sits like a tangled nest on her head. Her skin looks ashen. She is seated on the toilet, naked, with her knees apart, reaching a finger inside herself, as if removing a diaphragm. How odd. Since when do pregnant women practice birth control?

'What are you doing there?'

'Nothing.'

'You appear to be, um —'

'Can't a girl have any privacy?'

'This is our wedding day, Christine, and I —'

She flashes a smile. 'Oh, Hankypoo, I'm sorry. I just want a little privacy, okay?'

Steel yourself, man, and do it: speak up.

'Chris,' he says, shaking. Be strong! He deepens his voice. 'Tell me, Christine, have you been faithful to me?'

'What?'

'I need to know.'

'You're the one who fucked around, remember? The night you left me. Remember?'

'You slept with someone else,' he says bitterly.

Chris rolls her eyes. 'Who? You tell me, Mr. Know-It-All.'

But Hank cannot bring himself to ask her if she slept with Mike Blitsky. The thought alone is too repulsive. If he says it, and it isn't true, she will never forget it and he will never forgive himself. Better to draw the truth out of her, whatever it may be.

He says, 'Just tell me, is there any possibility this is not my child?'

A nasty grimace pinches her face. 'Oh, fuck it,' she says. She bends over and reaches up into herself. He hears the muted popping sound of a diaphragm in sudden release.

'Here,' she says. 'You wanted to see this so bad, it's yours!' Hank steps back as her goopy diaphragm comes sailing at him. It slaps against his forehead. Chris jumps up from the toilet, wimpering apologies, and rushes to him. She tries to hug him but he pulls away.

'Just tell me this,' he demands. 'Why did you use a diaphragm if you're pregnant?'

'I dunno, honey, just because. Oh, Hank, I would never be unfaithful to you, never. You're just tense because of the wedding.'

Hank appears to accept her reassurances: he takes a shower, and makes her favorite pancakes for breakfast. But doubt echoes in his beleagured mind. Shut alone in the bathroom, he rereads the letter numerous times and asks himself if it could possibly be true. He recalls the slap of the diaphragm against his forehead like the suction-kiss of a nasty ghost. All the sleazy remarks Blitsky ever made in passing haunt his cobwebby brain. He may be a complete dope in matters of love, but somewhere deep inside him, he knows that things are very wrong. If only he could take some action and save himself. He reasons that there is still some time to decide. Six hours and twenty-seven minutes, to be exact.

Noon. Wedding day. Hank knows he's cutting it close, but he had to come here; he has to find out the truth. He waits outside Blitsky's door in the vestibule of the twenty-second floor penthouse. The walls, ceiling and doors are painted like a blue and green swirling ocean, an aquamarine chaos that smacks of the sixties. Hank feels claustrophobic, standing in this manic colorful cube. He thinks that a mural of soothing dark space, twinkling with a few stars maybe, would better describe the New Age butt end of the twentieth century. Or maybe just a nice Miro print. He paces. Why don't they answer the door?

Finally, he hears footsteps and the metal scrape of someone sliding the peephole cover. After a moment the door opens. There is Roger, tall, cocoa-skinned and wearing only a pair of black bikini underpants and a red fishnet T-shirt.

'Well, hey!' Roger says. He calls behind his shoulder, 'It's your lawyer.' He shuts the door and leads Hank through the huge foyer with its checkerboard floor, to a massive living room decked out in overstuffed leather couches and chairs, heavy glass tables, colored Venetian glass candelabrum and two gold spray-painted lawn flamingos. A wall of sliding glass doors leads to a garden balcony, beyond which is a stunning panoramic view of Central Park and the east side. Hank hadn't known that his client lived quite so sumptuously.

Blitsky, wearing a chartreuse and magenta striped robe, is sunk into a plush white couch. Sitting next to him is an older man with a halo of white hair. The man is wearing a work shirt and denim overalls. When he opens his mouth, silver flashes.

'Welcome!' Blitsky says. 'You are a workaholic, Hank, aren't you. We were about to start dressing for your wedding.'

'I have to talk to you,' Hank says. He stands in the middle of the gigantic room, next to a gold flamingo.

'This is Mel Katz,' Mike introduces the older man. 'We just ordered up brunch. Join us?'

Mel Katz? Or is it really Mel Blitsky? Or is it really Mike Katz? Hank is sure this is the man in the photo. With those teeth, how could he not be?

'Would you like an espresso?' Roger asks Hank.

'No, thank you. I need to talk to you, Mike, privately. I don't have much time.'

'No,' Mike says, 'you don't.' He hoists himself up from the couch and says, 'We'll be in the library, Rog, if you need me.'

As they leave the room, Hank hears Mel saying to Roger: 'Kid's heading for the altar today? God save him . . . .'

Mike leads Hank through a dining-room with oxblood walls and a large oval table surrounded by Bauhaus chairs of chrome and black leather, down a wide hallway lined with posed photographs of Men, and into a room whose walls are covered with bookshelves. But there are no books. The shelves are crowded with toys: wind-ups, slinkies, puppets, stuffed animals, Gumbies. Red, yellow, green and purple bean bag chairs litter the floor.

'Have a seat,' Mike says. He plops down into one of the bean bags.

Hank can't bring himself to sit in one of those ridiculous seats. He is a real man, a professional, a serious thinker. He stands.

'That man is your father!' Hank announces. 'And you have violated my trust!' He whips out the envelope and hands it to Mike.

Mike cautiously opens the letter. When he sees the photo, he smiles. 'Oh Goddess, it *is* Dad!' He giggles. 'Where did you get this?'

'Mike, I want to know what is going on. Please read the letter. I need to know the exact truth.'

'Ah, the *exact* truth.' Mike nods, amused, and reads the letter. When he is finished, he looks up at Hank and asks, 'What does this picture have to do with the letter?'

'You tell me.'

'I haven't the foggiest,' he says. 'This picture is Dad, my brothers and me in our front yard. My stepmother Nellie took it. Where did you get it?'

Hank says, 'It came with the letter. As if you didn't know.'

'I didn't write this letter. Were I to write a confession — which, I assure you, I would not — it would be much more evocative. I would not write,' he reads: '"I slept with Chris Lustgarden. It was in July." I would say something more along the lines of,' he thinks, then says: '"One hot summer evening, as I strolled the moonlit shore of Cannes, I came upon a seething naked female, Chris, who gave herself to me in lust. If this mermaid is to be your wife, I both congratulate and pity you. But true love, lust does not cast asunder—"'

'Mike!' Frustration grips Hank's throat, strangling him. He must get to the bottom of this. He has things to do: either change into his tuxedo, or cancel the wedding. 'Did you write this letter?'

'What you're asking me is if I slept with your girl. I did not. I haven't slept with a woman in decades. Nor did I write this.' He flaps the letter in the air. 'How it came together with this picture, I most surely do not know.'

'Then who wrote it?' Hank pleads. 'Who wrote it? I'm going out of my mind. I need to know what this is all about!' Hank paces. Anguish is like dynamite in his head, like a dozen cups of coffee, like speed, like exhaustion, like....

'Hank, please sit down, please relax. Let's think this through rationally. You helped me when I was in trouble, now I think I can help you. Clearly, matters of love are not your forte. They happen to be mine. Sit.'

Hanks stops pacing. He looks at Mike.

'Sit down,' Mike says.

Hank obeys, lowering himself onto a bean bag. 'What am I going to do?'

'I may know the culprit.' Mike looks at the photo.

'Funny how things work out.'

'What are you talking about?'

'These are my brothers, Nathan and Mark. I haven't seen Nathan in years and years, I don't know where he is. I didn't know where Dad was until the book came out. It drew him out of the woodwork, happily I might add. He was right over there in Brooklyn all along! My father loves me,' Mike says, his eyes watering. 'Excuse me. I cry just like a girl, I always have, I can't help it. I just never thought Dad would accept me after, well, you know, all this. He hasn't said a word to me about my business. He accepts Roger just like a daughter. I can't tell you how happy I am, it's beyond my wildest dreams. We've been out of touch for twenty years. He doesn't know where Nathan is, either. And Mark, well, Mark resurfaced in my life a few years ago. He's a bit of a chameleon. I shouldn't be telling you all this, you being on the side of the law.'

'I'm not here professionally,' Hank says. 'I'm here purely on a personal level.'

'A social visit.' Mike smiles. 'Shall I reveal all to you? Truth tell?'

'I just want to know about Chris. Tell me whatever you know about the letter.'

'What do I know? To be perfectly frank, I think you're looking for a way out of this wedding. I think this letter is beside the point. I think you're in love with —'

'You're wrong!' Hank barks. 'I'm simply investigating this letter. I want to know who wrote it.'

'Okay. But I don't necessarily know anything about it, you understand, I simply have my suspicions. You've met my brother Mark.'

'No, I haven't.'

'You met him at my victory party. He was with you and Chris. He came with her.'

'You mean Marco, the temp?'

'Exactly. But he ain't no Marco and he ain't no temp. At least, he doesn't have to be. He's my brother and business partner, neither of which he can really stand. His whole life is about denial. Aliases. Phony professions. He needs to be out there in the workaday world with every other Tom, Dick and Harry, pretending to be just another stuffed shirt, a regular working guy. I don't understand it, really. He has a fabulous place on West Tenth Street. He collects art deco furniture, the genuine article. But he never entertains. He's terrified some-one will find out how he makes his real money. And person-ally, I think that his compulsion to conquer women is his way of denying how he earns his living.'

'Is he a Man?'

Mike laughs. 'Mark? He's strictly my manager. He handles advertising, investments and payroll. I take care of personnel and client relations.' He winks. 'He gets a share of the profits.'

'Why didn't you tell me you had a partner? I was your attorney. I could have gotten into big trouble not knowing something so central to your situation.'

Mike smiles wryly. 'I thought this was a social visit.'

And then the awful thought strikes Hank that this same man in question — this Mark, this Marco, the temp — had an affair with Dawn, and by her own admission. His very own Dawn, his beloved former fiancee. Mike is too right: he is in love with her, but what can he do? His mind ticks. Maybe get-ting this letter was not as terrible as it first seemed. Maybe it will prove to be the major boon of his life (beside his recent partnership). Maybe he can justifiably call off the wedding if he has a non-refutable and dramatic piece of evidence against Chris. It would have to be something that points out her abso-lute unsuitability to be his wife. Something like this letter, and its source. But damning Chris with Mark/Marco damns Dawn. She could have caught all kinds of evil diseases from a man who works with Men. What other dangers has she encoun-tered since he cast her out into the single life?

Frantically, Hanks asks, 'Is your brother having an affair with Christine?'

Mike shrugs. 'I don't know. Maybe.'

'He wrote this letter?'

'When did you get it? I see there's no postmark.'

'This morning, under my door.'

'Well, my friend, there goes that theory. Mark is in Swit-zerland at the moment, doing some private banking for the business.'

Hank says, 'Is that where —'

'I couldn't let the law confiscate it, could I?'

Hank holds back what blasts through his mind: you bastard, you jeopardized my career by withholding vital information! Instead, he says, 'If your brother didn't write this, then who the hell did?'

'And how did they get this picture?' Mike adds. 'And what on earth do they mean by this P.S.? What are we to make of the letter and picture, together? I most definitely do not know.'

'Well,' Hank sighs, 'neither do I. I'm totally confused. I have no idea what's going on. I'm getting married in a few hours and I have no solid reason to distrust Chris.' Except for that diaphragm business this morning, he thinks. 'She's supposed to be pregnant,' he mutters. 'I don't know, I just don't know.'

'A little Hank?' Mike says. 'How cute!'

'Well, I'm beginning to have my doubts.'

'Aha. A shotgun wedding with no ammunition.'

'Anyway, it's really better if she isn't pregnant. It doesn't mean we have to cancel the wedding. We can still get married, but without the added burden of children right away. That's perfectly reasonable.'

'You are blowing my little mind! You may not want to hear it, but I keep getting the impression that you've completely rationalized yourself into this whole situation.'

Hank shrugs. 'I don't know what I want, that's my problem. At the moment I just want the truth. Someone's tormenting me. Who? I want to know who?'

Poor Hank, tormenting himself when the truth is so obvious that even a fortune cookie knew to tell him to look within for his own worst enemy.

But will he?

Twenty-Four
Just Say No

'What a shoddy elevator!' Dawn moans to Randy. She wears a white chiffon dress with a tiny pink rose on an embroidered collar. Her hair is twisted into a *chignon,* woven with a sprig of lacy white Baby's Breath. She wafts with Chanel's *Coco.* On her wrist she wears a diamond bracelet (a gift from Hank on the second anniversary of their first date).

'You look like the bride yourself,' Randy says. He bends to kiss her cheek. She moves away.

"Not now, Randy, please.'

'The loft is probably nice,' he tries.

'I doubt it.'

The elevator in this renovated Chelsea warehouse is small and dim. The stainless steel walls are covered with greasy fingerprints. Dawn would never let her guests make such a downgrade entrance to her own wedding. But this is not her wedding, it's Hank's wedding. Suddenly, doubts surface about her decision to come here today. What's the point? What is she proving, and to whom? Her stubborn judgment that not coming would somehow weaken her now seems absurd. Hank is getting married, period, whether she watches or not. And she will be hurt, whether she watches or not. She decides to decide, first thing Monday, if she should call her old therapist for an appointment. She clutches her gift to the wedding couple: a Dustbuster, with the price tag still on it, wrapped in turquoise Macy's paper with the store's silver sticker right smack in the middle. On a tiny florist's card, Dawn crossed out *Merry Christmas* and typed in *On Your Wedding Day, Best Regards, Dawn Waterston and Randy Banks.*

The door slides open at the fifth floor. Suddenly they are in an enormous, elegant loft. Huge windows overlook Fifth Avenue. A string quartet plays Vivaldi's *Four Seasons.* Oversized vases sprout with branches of miniature white orchids. Yard-long candles flicker with honey-drop flames. One side of the space is set up with folding chairs facing an arbor decorated with pink roses and white lilies. Close to two hundred people mingle comfortably in the other half of the loft.

Dawn says, 'Where did she get this wedding, out of *Vogue?*'

'Let's get you a drink,' says Randy. 'Where should I put this box?'

'Anywhere invisible,' she says, wishing she were anywhere but here.

So many people! From within the galaxy of strangers she begins to see a constellation of faces from her old life with Hank. His boss, Grey Lesser and his wife Margaret; Mary McNeil, Hank's colleague who they used to have dinner with; his sister Becky with some guy Dawn has never seen before; his brother James with Cynthia, long-term live-ins who never married despite having two sons. This is really awful. They were her in-law-equivalents for three years. What is she to them now?

Dawn is relieved to see Randy maneuvering through the crowd with her red wine and his vodka and soda. She craves that glass of wine like an alcoholic; she would do anything to blot herself out at this moment. But before Randy is halfway across the room, Kath appears from behind a pillar and greets him. Jack is close behind. He's wearing his tuxedo, and Kath looks fabulous a ribbed, blue minidress that hugs contours Dawn never realized were there. She's even wearing makeup, and looks uncharacteristically stunning. Dawn, in comparison, feels like a school marm, a spinster, the ne'er wedded elder sister doomed to spend her free time knitting afghans for nieces and nephews.

Randy waves Dawn over, and she starts to cross the room. Just into the thick of the crowd, she hears, 'Dawn! Oh, Dawn!'

She turns around and there is Mrs. Lowe: a tall, once-pretty woman who is now handsome and elegant. Her salt-and-pepper pageboy haircut bounces as she hurries to Dawn. One enormous shoulder pad of her black silk dress has slipped by her breast. Dawn can't help wondering why a mother would wear black to her son's wedding.

'Liz,' Dawn says. 'How are you?'

Liz Lowe stands in front of Dawn, her shoulder pads all askew, smiling and shaking her head. 'You look just gorgeous, dear. You should be the bride.'

'Oh, Liz. You look great. Is Henry, Sr. here?'

'Oh, he's here, wandering around, looking down cleavage no doubt.' Then her face goes serious, falling from all smile lines into frowns. She leans toward Dawn. 'I'm so sorry, dear. I mean that, from the very bottom of my heart. If it makes you feel any better, we don't like her at all. We still think of you as our daughter-in-law.'

'Thanks, Liz. I'll always feel close to you and Henry.' But Dawn's no dummy; she knows perfectly well that after this wedding, she will probably never see the Lowe family again.

'Will you excuse me?' Dawn says. 'My friend is waiting for me.'

Liz hugs and kisses Dawn, and whispers, 'Chin up.'

Dawn escapes to Randy, Kath and Jack.

'The big day,' Kath says, rolling her eyes. 'This is hard to believe.'

'I saw him in the back room.' Jack shakes his head. 'I dunno, I just don't know.'

'What did you get them?' Dawn asks.

Kath says, 'Place mats,' and shrugs.

'There's Andy Shoemaker,' says Dawn. 'Who's he with?'

Kath looks with great interest. Andy's new woman is plump and wears a green-flowered dress, with four-inch heels and teased hennaed hair.

'Must be his secretary,' Dawn says. They all laugh.

Andy comes over with his date and introduces her as Gloria. She bats her thickly mascaraed eyelashes. 'Hi, how are ya?'

'Gloria's an Assistant Vice President in our public financing division,' Andy says.

Dawn smiles. 'Really? How exciting.'

'Eh, it's a living,' Gloria says. 'I need another Perrier. You wanna get another round,' she asks Andy, 'or should I?'

'Allow me. Anyone else need a refill?'

All decline. Andy takes Gloria's glass and goes off to the bar. Just as he disappears, Mike Blitsky, arm-in-arm with Roger, fills his place. They are dressed in suits which are identical except in color: Mike's is silver, Roger's is red.

Mike kisses Dawn once on each cheek, and softly says, 'Don't you look lovely!' Greetings are traded as he kisses Kath and Jack. To Gloria, he says, 'How beautiful. You are a stunning lady, to be sure.' He bows, and kisses the back of her hand, with its extra-long red fingernails.

Gloria says, 'Hey, you the guy wrote that book? I'm reading it. Wow!'

''Tis I,' says Mike. He hands her a card. 'Visit me at any time and I will autograph your copy with my own semen.'

'Yeah, thanks.' She slips the card into her green sequined handbag.

Andy reappears with his Scotch and her Perrier. 'Twist of lime,' he says, handing her the glass.

And then he sees Mike. And Mike sees him. And their gazes lock like magnets. Andy raises his eyebrows and sips his drink, but his sudden pallor escapes no one, nor does his unsteady hand.

A huge smile blossoms on Mike's face, and he is about to speak when the string quartet changes its tune to the opening phrases of the wedding march. The guests move in a tidal wave to the other half of the loft, separating Andy and Mike, and abruptly shifting attention from what might have become a significant confrontation, to the main event.

Seated, Dawn's view is obscured by a sea of mousse-fluffed hairdos. Blood surges through her as the room falls to silence. Here it is: the dreaded moment. Dawn takes Kath's hand and holds on tight.

The wedding march is in full swing now. Two bride's maids, in matching pale pink gowns, smile and glance around as they walk down the aisle. They are followed by Hank's brother James, the best man, and Ellen, the bride's maid, in an ivory lace gown. The bridal party gathers by the arbor, beaming.

Then comes Hank, who strides stiffly down the aisle, a lone soldier in a single-breasted tailcoat. He looks like a footman. Poor Hank, destined to be Chris's servant for life. Dawn stares at him. Her heart pounds. He looks exhausted. His skin is pale and his forehead is bunched with tension. Wake up, Hanky, wake up! she silently pleads. She starts to cry. Oh, Hank, please wake up and smell the coffee! He reaches the arbor and stands to the right, facing the guests, with his hands clasped, hog-tied, behind his back.

Here comes the bride, all dressed in white. Chris sashays bridally down the aisle in a low-cut lace gown with a long train held up by two little flower girls in matching pink dresses. Perched on her stiff black hair is a lace cap sprouting yards of white netting. She clutches a bouquet of pink roses, white lilies and Baby's Breath at her waist. The engagement ring glitters on her finger.

Dawn's breath is shallow and quick, she feels like she's going to faint. 'Oh my God, oh my God,' she whispers to Kath.

'Shhh. It'll be over in a minute.'

Chris reaches the arbor. She looks at Hank and — is Dawn imagining it? — he looks at her grimly, with the eyes of the doomed.

Hank and Chris face the minister, their backs to the guests. The music stops. Silence. The minister speaks.

'We are gathered here today in the presence of family and friends, to witness the marriage of Christine and Henry. A wedding is a ceremony, it is a time of cheer and happiness, a cause for celebration. But let us not forget the solemn nature of the event, for it is an exchanging of vows, an intimate union of two lives, requiring the utmost of trust, faith and respect. Marriage at its best is a living organism, a state of flux, not just of happiness but of strife, and we must be flexible to its demands. When two people, such as Christine and Henry, choose to marry, they are choosing love over loneliness, family over solitude, and they relinquish their separate worlds for one shared universe. No longer is it possible to sustain individual lives, to live selfishly meeting only one's own needs and wants, for they have merged into a new and different life together. Married life. It is at once the best and most difficult state in which two people can live. For Christine and Henry, this day is the beginning of a journey which will last the rest of their lives. Let us all pause now in a moment of silent prayer for them.'

Heads bow. Dawn, for one, skips the prayer and goes right for the jugular. *That nasty bitch,* she thinks, *I hope she dies in childbirth.*

The minister says, 'Is there any man or woman in this room who objects to this union? If so, let him speak now or forever hold his peace.'

Silence.

'Then let us proceed. The rings, please.'

Ellen hands Chris Hank's ring. James gives Hank Chris's.

'Christine Eleanor Lustgarden, do you take Henry Maxwell Lowe, Jr. to be your wedded husband, promising to love and cherish him, in health and in sickness, for better or . worse, til death do you part?'

'I do.'

'Henry Maxwell Lowe, Jr., do you take Christine Eleanor Lustgarden to be your wedded wife, promising to love and cherish her, in health and in sickness, for beter or worse, til death do you part?'

Hank does not respond.

'Henry?' says the minister.

Chris glares at Hank, her eyes wide, her lips tight. She whispers, 'Hank!'

'No,' he says, just like that: 'No.'

Guests mumble in shock and confusion. Dawn bursts into tears.

Hank says, 'I'm sorry, but I can't.' His face is bright red.

'Fuck you!' Chris screams. She races down the aisle, followed by Ellen and the bride's maids.

People remain seated. The din heightens. No one knows what to do: does one leave, or stay for the food?

Mike Blitsky stands and whistles.

Jack shouts: 'Atta boy!'

Laughter erupts.

Hank stands by the arbor, frantically searching the sea of guests.

Dawn's eyes are pinned on him. She's terrified. Is this real, or just one of her fantasies come to life? In her panic, she cannot see that, for once, the trickster Fate is playing in her favor.

When Hank spots her, he rushes down the aisle chanting, *'Dawn, Dawn.'*

She bolts up, and pushes past Kath's and Jack's knees. Shaking, crying, she stands in the aisle as Hank rushes to her.

The next few moments feel like slow motion: standing there, vulnerable, with all these people watching Hank moving toward her, his face aflame, his tuxedo tails flapping behind him, his arms reaching for her as he nears. She steps forward and they collide. As they kiss, the room breaks into cheers and applause.

Hank falls to his knees. Clutching the hem of her white dress, he implores, 'Marry me, *please*'

The bridal bouquet comes sailing down the aisle, aimed straight at the back of Dawn's head. Just in the nick of time, she turns around, sees it, and lifts a grasping hand.

ABOUT THE AUTHOR

Katia Lief is an international bestselling novelist. She teaches fiction writing at The New School in Manhattan and lives in Brooklyn. Learn more at katialief.com